Mary Whitney Morrison

**Songs and Rhymes for the Little Ones**

Mary Whitney Morrison

**Songs and Rhymes for the Little Ones**

ISBN/EAN: 9783337273088

Printed in Europe, USA, Canada, Australia, Japan

Cover: Foto ©Andreas Hilbeck / pixelio.de

More available books at **www.hansebooks.com**

# SONGS AND RHYMES

FOR

# THE LITTLE ONES

COMPILED BY

MARY WHITNEY MORRISON

(JENNY WALLIS)

New Edition

WITH AN INTRODUCTION

BY MRS. A. D. T. WHITNEY

BOSTON
JOSEPH KNIGHT COMPANY
1896

# INTRODUCTION.

## To the Mothers, Aunts, and Grandmothers of the Little Ones.

One might almost as well offer June roses with the assurance of their sweetness, as so to present this lovely little gathering of verse, which announces itself, like them, by its own deliciousness. Yet, as Mrs. Morrison's charming volume has long been a delight to me, I am only too happy to link my name with its new and enriched form in this slight way, and simply declare that it is to me, — and to two families of my grandchildren, who have had a copy of the first edition all read to pieces for them in their nursery days, — the most bewitching book of songs for little people that we have ever known.

And it is not fair, either, to speak of it as only for the little people. It has made many a charming holiday hour for the elder readers, who find in its pages a keen, delicate wit and meaning, and a grace of musical versification, that are an inspiration to vocal rendering, and a source of enduring pleasure that repetition never wearies.

It is, in short, a most choice budget of happy rhymes, which will surely sing themselves into all hearts, and abide as household words in every home.

ADELINE D. T. WHITNEY.

MILTON HILL, July, 1895.

# NOTE.

It has been a labor of love to collect these poems, for the instruction and amusement of the dear children of our home circle. They have made many a rainy day bright with mirth, have lightened days of illness, and dried the tears from loved eyes of every hue, — each dear to the parent heart. I have been urged to share these pleasures with others, and now present this volume to the public, hoping that in each home of our loved land it may prove a blessing.

> For babies dear,
> And children small;
> For lads and lassies,
> Short and tall;
> For bright black eyes.
> And tender blue,
> I bring my gifts,
> Both old and new.

M. W. M.

THE compiler's gratitude is due, and is hereby expressed, for the kindness of many authors and publishers in allowing the use of their poems, especially to Houghton, Mifflin & Co., Harper & Brothers, Chas. Scribner's Sons, and the Century Company, to whom she is deeply indebted.

# CONTENTS.

# CONTENTS.

# SONGS AND RHYMES

## FOR THE LITTLE ONES.

---

### AN AUTUMN JINGLE.

I KNOW a little creature in a green bed,
   With the softest wrappings all around her head,
When she grows old, she is hard and cannot feel,
So they take her to the mill, and make her into meal.

---

### LITTLE GOLDEN HAIR.

LITTLE Golden-hair, with Fritz,
   See how quietly he sits,
Playing with his Christmas toys,
Is he not the best of boys?

Little Golden-hair one day
Went to walk, and lost his way,
How we all were worried then,
But Fritz brought him home again.

## LITTLE JILL HORNER.

LITTLE Jill Horner,
    She sat in the corner,
Eating her birthday cake;
With fingers and thumbs,
She then picked up the crumbs,
That Jack had helped her to make.

JENNY WALLIS.

## LITTLE TEDDY.

OUR boy Teddy,
    Sitting in the tub,
Take the soap and flannel,
And give the boy a rub.

Turning up his little toes,
Cocking up his little nose,
Our boy Teddy,
Sitting in a tub.

## WEE WILLIE WINKIE.

WEE Willie Winkie running through the town,
    Up stairs and down stairs in his night gown;
Tapping at the window, trying at the lock,
All the babes are in their beds, for now 't is ten o'clock.

Wee Willie Winkie, are you coming then?
The cat's singing briskly to the sleeping hen,
The dog lies stretched upon the hearth, I would not gie
      a cheep,
For he's a wakeful laddie, that will not go to sleep.

---

## THE SPECKLEDY HEN.

SPECKLEDY hen! Speckledy hen!
    What do you do in my garden pen?
Mother will scold you, you know she will,
And father will beat you for doing ill;
And I'd like to know what you'll do then,
You dear little naughty speckledy hen?

---

## SONG OF THE LITTLE RED HEN.

CLUCK, cluck, cluck,
    I'm glad I'm not a duck;
Weet, weet, weet,
For then I'd have web feet;
Clack, clack, clack,
And water on my back;
Trill, trill, trill,
And such a vulgar bill.
But now I've eight free toes,
And lovely Roman nose;
Cluck, cluck, cluck,
I'm glad I'm not a duck.

## THE LITTLE COCK SPARROW.

A LITTLE cock sparrow sat on a high tree,
   And he chirrupped, he chirrupped so merrily.

A naughty little boy with a bow and arrow
Determined to shoot this little cock sparrow.

For this little cock sparrow would make a nice stew,
And his giblets would make a nice little pie too.

"Oh, no," says cock sparrow, "I won't make a stew,"
And he fluttered his wings and away he flew.

—◆—

## NURSERY RHYME.

JENNY WREN fell sick
   Upon a merry time,
In came Robin Redbreast
   And brought her sops of wine.

Eat well of the sop, Jenny,
   Drink well of the wine;
Thank you Robin kindly,
   You shall be mine.

Jenny she got well,
   And stood upon her feet,
And told Robin plainly
   She loved him not a bit.

Robin, being angry,
   Hopped upon a twig,
Saying, "Out upon you,
   Fie upon you, bold faced jig."

———

## THE PIN.

TALL and slender, straight and thin,
   Shining, useful little pin ;
The Graces, knowing well your worth,
Themselves have sent you down to earth ;
Devoted to the female race,
To give each fold its proper place,
To bind the slender tapering waist,
And dress each lovely form with taste.

———

## ANNIE'S NURSERY SONG.

HERE sits the Lord Mayor,
   Here sit his two men,
Here sits the cock,
And here sits the hen,
Here sit the chickens,
And here they go in,
Chippety, chippety, chippety chin.

Touching the baby in turn on forehead, eyes, cheeks, nose, mouth,
and under the chin.

# A RAINY DAY SONG.

DEAR little tippy-toes,
　　Dear little nippy-nose,
Little hands and feet,
Dimpled, sweet, sweet, sweet;
Little rosy lips, and baby eyes brown,
Go to sleep, dearie, while the rain comes down.


　　Old mother Henny Hen,
　　Little mother Jenny Wren,
　　Take their babies small,
　　Little wee ones all;
Cover them up snug, for fear they will drown,
Under warm feathers, while the rain comes down.


　　Mrs. Red Mooly Cow,
　　Under an apple-bough
　　Moos to her calf —
　　So frisky, you'd laugh —
Stands in the meadow, where the grass is mown,
Keeps her baby safe, while the rain comes down.


　　Gray-coated Kitty Cat,
　　Gives little kits a pat;
　　Don't want one to get
　　Furry soft paws wet.
So she purrs gently, keeps them till they're grown,
Safe under shelter, while the rain comes down.

So little tippy-toes,
Dear little nippy-nose,
Baby eyes so clear,
Shut them up, my dear,
Cuddle up close in your fair white gown,
Mother'll hold you, darling, while the rain comes down.

---

## ROBINS LEARNING TO FLY.

TWO robin-redbreasts built their nest
    Within a hollow tree,
The hen sat quietly at home,
    The cock sang merrily,
And all the little young ones said,
    "Wee, wee,--- wee, wee,— wee, wee!"

One day the sun was warm and bright,
    And cloudless was the sky,
Cock-robin said, "My little dears,
    'T is time you learned to fly."
And all the little young ones said,
    "I'll try, I'll try, I'll try!"

I know a child, and who she is
    I'll tell you by and by:
When mamma says, "Do this, do that,"
    She says, "What for?" and "Why?"
She'd be a better child by far,
    If she would say, "I'll try."

*Aunt Effie's Rhymes.*

## KINDNESS TO THE BIRDS.

WHENEVER I see, on bush or tree,
    Young birds in their little nest,
I must not, in my play, steal the birds away,
    Or grieve their mother's breast.

My mother, I know, would sorrow so,
    If I should be stolen away ;
So I 'll speak to the birds in my softest words,
    Nor harm them in my play.

—◆—

## THE TIRED SEAMSTRESS.

MAMMA, I 've lost my thimble,
    And my spool has rolled away,
My arm is aching dreadfully,
    And I want to go and play.

There 's Johnny playing marbles,
    And Susie skipping rope,
They 've finished all their easy tasks,
    While I must sit and mope.

If I could set the fashion,
    I know what I would do,
I 'd not be troubling people
    To sit so still and sew ;

I'd put some homespun on their necks,
  And sew it all around,
And make them look like cotton bags,
  Placed endwise on the ground.

Mamma, she's gone and left me,
  And closely shut the door,
Mamma, mamma, come back again,
  I will not grumble more.

---

## NURSERY RHYME.

THERE was an old woman, as I've heard tell,
  She went to the market her eggs for to sell;
She went to market all on a market day;
And she fell asleep on the king's highway.

There came by a pedler whose name was Stout,
He cut her petticoats all round about;
He cut her petticoats up to her knees,
Which made the old woman to shiver and freeze.

When this little woman first did wake,
She began to shiver, and she began to shake;
She began to wonder, and she began to cry,
"Lauk-a-mercy on me, this is none of I:

"But if it be I, as I do hope it be,
I've a little dog at home, and he'll know me;
If it be I, he'll wag his little tail,
And if it be not I, he'll loudly bark and wail!"

Home went the little woman all in the dark,
Up got the little dog, and he began to bark;
He began to bark, so she began to cry,
"Lauk-a-mercy on me, this is none of I!"

---◆---

## BESSIE'S KIND CRUELTY.

IN garments white, and ribbons blue,
    Our Bessie to the barnyard flew;
There pretty, downy chickens seven,
    Their mother fed from morn till even. ·

"I love ou so!" the maiden cried,
    And hugged and kissed one till it died;
And so with many a hug and kiss,
    She proved, alas, a cruel miss.

The hen quite wild and furious grew,
    Of chicks alive she had but two;
"Cluck, cluck! cluck, cluck!" she cried in vain,
    "Of friends like these I must complain."

Now, when you wish your love to show,
    Please stop a bit, until you know
What best will please the one you love,
    And thus a true affection prove.

JENNIE WALLIS.

## ALL THE SAME IN THE END.

LITTLE black Dinah, she sits in her chair,
   Staring at Lily, so dainty and fair.
Little black Dinah is wond'ring, may be,
"What is the name of that little pale baby?"
Little Miss Lily cannot understand
Why that little girl is so "awfully tanned."

In the two little noddles, so wondrously wise,
Are a pair of round black, and a pair of blue eyes,—
In each little body a child's pure heart,
And a white, white soul, of heaven a part;
And oh, one day, in the heaven above,
They will both be sharing a Saviour's love.

MARY D. BRINE.

## FISHING.

THREE small children were fishing,
   Fishing with rod and line;
One was three, and one was six,
   And one was nearly nine.

What do you think they fished for?
   One of them really thought,
Out of a nurs'ry window,
   Real live fish could be caught.

One of them just pretended
    Fish could be caught that way ;
He stood by the window and listened,
    Just because it was play.

One of them thought 't was funny
    Because the others wished,
So she stood with her brothers,
    And that's the way they fished.

---

## LITTLE DAISY.

WAKE up, little daisy, the summer is nigh,
    The dear little robin is up in the sky ;
The snowdrops and crocus were never so slow,
Then wake up, little daisy, and hasten to grow ;
    Wake up !
Wake up, little daisy, and hasten to grow.

I tease pleasant sunshine to rest on your head,
The dew and the raindrops to moisten your bed,
And then every morning I just take a peep,
To see your little face, but you 're still fast asleep ;
    Wake up !
Wake up, little daisy, and hasten to grow.

Listen, little daisy, and I 'll tell you what 's said,
The lark thinks you 're lazy, and love your warm bed,
But I 'll not believe it, for now I can see
Your bright little eye winking softly at me ;
    Wake up !
Wake up, little daisy, and hasten to grow.

## JINGLE.

LITTLE Miss Dorothy Do
    Went down the street, I'd have you know,
In her mother's long-trained dinner-dress,
And she cut a queer figure, as you may guess.

She wore her sister's velvet hat,
And her auntie's travelling bag ; and that
Was not enough, for she borrowed, too,
Her grandmother's veil so long and blue.

She walked until she was ready to drop,
And fell asleep in a candy shop,
What she did next I did n't hear,
But I'll let you know when I do, my dear.

MARY D. BRINE.

## TREE ON THE HILL.

ON yonder hill there stands a tree ;
    Tree on the hill, and the hill stood still.

And on the tree there was a branch ;
Branch on the tree, tree on the hill, and the hill stood
        still.

And on the branch there was a nest ;
Nest on the branch, branch on the tree, tree on the hill,
        and the hill stood still.

And in the nest there was an egg;
Egg in the nest, nest on the branch, branch  on  the  tree,
      tree on the hill, and the hill stood still.

And in the egg there was a bird;
Bird in  the  egg,  egg  in  the  nest,  nest  on  the  branch,
      branch  on  the  tree,  tree  on  the  hill,  and  the
      hill  stood  still.

And on the bird there was a feather;
Feather  on  the  bird,  bird  in  the  egg,  egg  in  the  nest,  nest
      on  the  branch,  branch  on  the  tree,  tree  on  the
      hill,  and  the  hill  stood  still.

---

## THE BLACKSMITH MAN.

MY mother puts an apron on, to keep my coaties clean,
    And  rubbers  on  my  little  boots,  and  then  I  go  and
    lean
Against the blacksmith's  doorway,  to  watch  the  coal  fire
    shine.
The bellows heave, the hammers swing — I wish they were
    all mine!
The  horses  bend  their  legs  and  stand;  I  don't  see  how
    they can;
But I would love to shoe their feet, just like the black-
    smith man.
    Tang-tiddle, tang-tiddle, tang-tiddle-tan!
    What a jolly noise he makes, the blacksmith man!

When I grow up an old, big man, with whiskers on my chin,
I will not have a grocery store, or dry-goods store, or tin ;
I will not be a farmer, or a lawyer, not a bit :
Or President,— all the other boys are meaning to be it —
Or a banker, with the money bills piled high upon the stan' —
I 'd rather hold the red-hot iron, and be a blacksmith man,
    Tang-tiddle, tang-tiddle, tang-tiddle-tan !
    Oh, what a jolly noise he makes, the blacksmith man !

The blacksmith man has got such arms ; his shop is such
        a place :
He gets as dirty as he likes, and no one cleans his face !
And when the lightning's in the sky he makes his bellows
        blow,
And all his fires flare quickly up, like lightning down
        below.
Oh, he must have the nicest time that any person can ;
I wish I could grow up to-day, and be a blacksmith man !
    Tang-tiddle, tang-tiddle, tang-tiddle-tan !
    I wish I could grow up to-day, and be a blacksmith man !

I mean to have a little house, with vines and porches to 't,
And fixed up nice and clean for me, when I get tired of soot.
I 'd marry little Susy, and have her for my wife —
We 've been so well acquainted with each other all our
        life !
Oh, I mean to be as hearty, and as happy as I can,
And an honest, good, hard-working, jolly, rosy blacksmith
        man !
    Tang-tiddle, tang-tiddle, tang-tiddle-tan !
    Here goes the honest, good, hard-working, jolly black-
        smith man !

# AMY'S ALPHABET.

A was the Apple so round and so red;
   B was the Bump as it fell on my head.
C was the Cry, that every one heard;
D was my Dolly, whose pity was stirred.
E was my Eye so blinded with tears;
F was my Face, now sad for my years.
G was my Grandmother, tender and tried;
H was her Handkerchief, which my tears dried.
I was the Ivy, that grew o'er the door;
J was the Jelly, that to me she bore.
K was the Knife, that she used for the cake;
L was the Lunch, that so soon she did make.
M was my Mother, who then came from town;
N was the Nut, that she brought me so brown.
O was the Orange from her pocket she took;
P was the Paper, that from it she shook.
Q was the Quail she had brought for my tea;
R was our Rover, who stole it from me.
S was my Sister, who soon brought it back;
T was the Turkey, whose bones we did crack.
U was my Uncle, who helped himself twice;
V was the Vane, that turned in a trice.
W the Wind, that blew down the tree;
Xactly how, I never could see.
You have listened so kindly that I must declare,
Zephyrs are really nothing but air.

JENNY WALLIS.

# PUSS AND HER THREE KITTENS.

OUR old cat has kittens three ;
    What do you think their names should be?
One is a tabby with emerald eyes,
   And a tail that 's long and slender ;
But into a temper she quickly flies,
   If you ever by chance offend her.
      I think we shall call her this —
        I think we shall call her that :
     Now, don't you fancy " Pepper-pot"
       A nice name for a cat ?

One is black, with a frill of white,
   And her feet are all white fur, too :
If you stroke her, she carries her tail upright,
   And quickly begins to purr, too.
      I think we shall call her this —
        I think we shall call her that :
     Now, don't you fancy " Sootikin "
       A nice name for a cat ?

One is a tortoise-shell, yellow and black,
   With a lot of white about him :
If you tease him, at once he sets up his back ;
   He 's a quarrelsome Tom, ne'er doubt him !
      I think we shall call him this —
        I think we shall call him that :
     Now, don't you fancy " Scratchaway"
       A nice name for a cat ?

Our old cat has kittens three,
And I fancy these their names will be :
    "Pepper-pot " — " Sootikin "— " Scratchaway."— There !
    Were there ever kittens with these to compare ?
And we call the old mother — now, what do you think ?
" Tabitha Longclaws Tidleywink ! "

THOMAS HOOD, Jr.

---

## KATIE'S LUNCHEON.

ONCE I had a little cake,
    Which mother in a tin did bake.

Twice I thought I 'd eat it up,
And drink the milk within my cup.

Three times I raised it to my lips,
And from my milk I took three sips.

Four times I peeped outside the door,
Where stood a little beggar poor.

Five times I thought, "I feel no need,
And this poor child is starved indeed. "

Six hasty steps I then did take,
And gave to her my little cake.

Seven smiles came quick, I gave her eight,
Nine times she said "Thank you, Miss Kate."

Ten times as happy now I feel,
Since I have shared with her my meal.

JENNY WALLIS.

## THREE IN A BED.

GRAY little velvet coats,
    One, two, three:
Any home happier
    Could there be?
Topsy and Johnny
    And sleepy Ned,
Purring so cosily,
    Three in a bed.


Woe to the stupid mouse,
    Prowling about!
Old Mother Pussy
    Is on the lookout:
Little cats, big cats,
    All must be fed,
In the sky parlor
    Three in a bed.


Mother's a gypsy puss;
    Often she moves,
Thinking much travel
    Her children improves.
High-minded family,
    Very well bred;
No falling out, you see!
    Three in a bed.

## THANK YOU, PRETTY COW.

THANK you, pretty cow, that made
    Pleasant milk to soak my bread,
Every day and every night,
Warm and sweet and fresh and white.

Do not chew the hemlock rank
Growing on the weedy bank;
But the yellow cowslip eat,
They will make it very sweet.

Where the bubbling water flows,
Where the purple violet grows,
Where the grass is fresh and fine,
Pretty cow, go there and dine.

JANE TAYLOR.

## KATIE'S WANTS.

ME want Christmas tree,
    Yes, me do;
Want an orange on it,
    Lots of candy too.

Want some new dishes,
    Want a red pail,
Want a rocking horse
    With a *very* long tail.

Want a little watch
  That says " Tick, tick!"
Want a newer dolly,
  'Cause Victoria's sick;

Want so many things
  Don't know what to do;
Want a little sister,
  Little brother too.

Won't you buy 'em, mamma?
  Tell me why you won't?
*Want to go to bed?*
  No, me don't.
                              Eva M. Tappan.

## POMP AND I.

POMP lies in one chair, I in another.
  (Pomp's a black cat, I'm his brother.)

There we be blinkin' in the sun,
Blinkin' and thinkin'— Oh! what fun!

What d'you suppose we're thinkin' 'bout?
One o' the things "no feller can't find out."

I'm so glad I'm nothing but a cat;
Pomp he says "that's so," to that.

Fat and lazy all day long,
Plenty to eat and can't do wrong.

When it comes to the end o' day,
We go to sleep on the bed o' hay.

All I can say is, I'm as happy as a cat;
"Happy as a clam" is nothin' to that.

---

## THE LITTLE MAID.

THERE was a little maid,
    And she had a little bonnet,
And she had a little finger,
With a little ring upon it.
And what's a little odd,
Her little heart was then
In love, but not a little,
With the best of little men;
For the little youth did exercise
His little flattering tongue,
And down before her little feet
His little knees he flung.
And he pressed her little hand,
In her little face he gazed,
And looked as though his little head
Was a very little crazed.
Alas! her little lover
Did with little warning leave her,
And she found him little better
Than a little gay deceiver;
So in a little moment,
(Stifling all her little wishes),

She took a little jump
All among the little fishes.
And now all little maidens
Whose little loves grow stronger,
Upon the little moral
Of this little tale may ponder.

Beware of little trinkets,
Little men and little sighs,
For you little know what great things
From little things may rise.

———◆———

## PAPA'S BABY.

NO little steps do I hear in the hall;
   Only a sweet silver laugh,— that is all;
No dimpled arms round my neck hold me tight,
I 've but a glimpse of two eyes very bright.
Two hands a wee little face try to screen;
Baby is hiding, that 's plain to be seen.
" Where is my precious I 've missed so all day?"
" Papa can't find me!" the pretty lips say.

"Dear me! I wonder where baby can be!"
Then I go by and pretend not to see.
" Not in the parlor, and not on the stairs!
Then I must peep under sofas and chairs."
The dear little rogue is now laughing outright.
Two little arms round my neck clasp me tight.
Home will indeed be sad, weary, and lone,
When papa can't find you, my darling, my own.

## A FUNNY FACT.

TADDY POLE, and Polly Wogg
Lived together in a bog:
Here you see the very pool,
Where they went to swimming-school.

By and by (it's true, but strange),
O'er them came a wondrous change:
Here you have them on a log,
Each a most decided frog.

———◆———

## THE PRETTY LITTLE MAIDEN.

A PRETTY little maiden
Had a pretty little dream,
And a pretty little wedding
Was its pretty little theme.

A pretty little bachelor
To win her favor tried,
And asked her how she'd like to be
His pretty little bride.

With some pretty little blushes,
And a pretty little sigh,
And a pretty little glance
From her pretty little eye,

From her pretty little face
Behind her pretty little fan,
She smiled on the proposals
Of this pretty little man.

Now this pretty little maiden
And her pretty little spark
Met the pretty little parson,
And his pretty little clerk,*

A pretty little wedding ring
United them for life,
And this pretty little husband
Had a pretty little wife.

## THE BOASTING HEN.

· "KE-DAW! Ke-daw!" a young hen cried,
      While strutting through a barnyard wide.
"Ke-daw Ke-daw!" I 've done a feat,
In chickendom it can't be beat!
I 've laid the finest egg to-day
That any hen in town could lay;
So, little chickens, far and near,
Just bow your head when I appear.
Old mother hens, you need n't sneer;
There never was an egg so white,
I shall go frantic with delight!"
"Ke-daw! Ke-daw!" rang clear and loud,
There never was a hen so proud.

* Pronounced clark.

The older hens were grave and staid.
They said, " When other eggs are laid —
Six or a dozen at the most —
My child, you won't care much to boast.
Your utterance will be more soothing
When laying eggs becomes no new thing."
Each turned and called away her brood.
This young hen thought their actions rude.
" How envious these old dames are !
My triumph, though, they shall not mar ;
With bitterness my heart would sicken
If I were such a jealous chicken."

Now, while this scene was going on,
Our dame had left her nest alone,
And, spying out a splended chance,
A weasel threw a furtive glance
At this same egg.

       Swift as a lance
He rolled it from its downy nest —
A wanton act be it confessed —
Its golden freshness there to test.

Back in high feather came our hen.
Her grief is not for tongue or pen !
She gazed upon the empty shell
Of that first egg she loved so well ;
Had she but known enough to cry,
Tears would have trickled from her eye.

Now in this egg-shell we may find
A simple moral left behind.

In boasting don't be premature,
Lest disappointment work your cure.
Ere you parade your triumph round,
Be sure your egg is safe and sound!

GEORGE COOPER.

---

## LITTLE DAME CRUMP.

LITTLE Dame Crump
    With her little hair broom,
One morning was sweeping
Her little bed-room.

When, casting her little
Gray eyes on the ground,
In a sly little corner
A penny she found.

"Odds Bobs!" cried the dame
While she stared with surprise,
"How lucky am I,
Bless my heart, what a prize!

"To market I'll go,
And a pig I will buy,
And little John Gubbins
Shall make him a sty."

She washed her face clean,
And put on her gown,
And locked up her house,
And set off for the town;

Where to market she went,
And a bargain she made ;
For a white little pig
The penny she paid.

Having purchased the pig,
She was puzzled to know
How they both should get home,
If the pig would not go.

So, fearing that piggy
Might play her a trick,
She drove him along
With a little crab-stick.

Piggy ran till he came
To the foot of a hill,
Where a little bridge stood
O'er the stream of a mill,

When he grunted and squeaked,
And no further would go :
Oh, fie little pig,
To serve the dame so !

She went to the miller's
And borrowed a sack,
Popped the little pig in,
And took on her back.

Piggy cried to get out,
But the little dame said,
"If you won't go by fair means
You then must be made."

So she carried the pig
To his nice little sty,
And made him a bed
Of clean straw, snug and dry.

With a handful of peas
Little pig she then fed,
And put on her night-cap,
And jumped into bed.

Having first said her prayers,
Then she put out her light,
And being quite tired,
We will bid her good-night.

———◆———

## THE SWEET LITTLE DOLL.

I ONCE had a sweet little doll, dears,
   The prettiest doll in the world.
Her cheeks were so red and so white, dears,
   And her hair was so charmingly curled.
And I lost my sweet little doll, dears,
   As I played on the heath one day,
And I cried for more than a week, dears,
   But I never could find where she lay.

And I found my sweet little doll, dears,
   As I played on the heath one day,
Folks say she is terribly changed, dears,
   For her paint is all washed away,

And her arms trodden off by the cows, dears,
And her hair, not the least bit curled,
But for old sake's sake, she is still, dears,
The prettiest doll in the world.

CHARLES KINGSLEY.

---

## THE SULKY OLEANDER.

LITTLE Oleander slip
    Cut from mother tree,
Was about as disagreeable
    As a little slip could be.
Did n't like her pot of earth;
    Said she would n't grow:
This was very naughty,
    And foolish too you know.

Little Oleander slip
    A drink of water had;
Did n't do her any good;
    Continued to be bad.
Sulky Oleander
    Hung her little head.
And, drooping over sideways,
    Pretended she was dead.

But it was n't any good
    Playing such a trick:
Tied up Oleander
    To a little stick;

Shut her in a closet,
　　Very dark, you know,
Till she made her mind up
　　To be good, and grow.

Darkness had a good effect
　　On Oleander's head ;
" What's the use of acting so ! "
　. To herself she said.
Straightened up her wilting stalk ;
　　Really tried to smile :
Guess we 'll have to let her out
　　In a little . while.

Morning bright and sunny,
　　Air so fresh and pure ;
Oleander's had enough
　　Of closet, I am sure ;
" Be good, Oleander ? "
　　" Yes," I heard her say,
And she 's kept her promise
　　From that very day.

Other little flowers
　　Sometimes act just so,
And in darkened closets
　　Often have to go.
There in calm reflection,
　　It will not be strange,
If a short confinement
　　Works a wondrous change.

*The Nursery.*

## A LITTLE BOY'S POCKET.

DO you know what's in my pottet?
    Such a lot of treasures in it!
Listen now while I bedin it:
Such a lot of sings it holds,
And everysin dats in my pottet,
And when, and where, and how I dot it.
First of all, here's in my pottet
A beauty shell, I pit'd it up:
And here's the handle of a tup
That somebody has broked at tea;
The shell's a hole in it, you see:
Nobody knows dat I dot it,
I teep it safe here in my pottet.
And here's my ball too in my pottet,
And here's my pennies, one, two, free,
That Aunty Mary dave to me,
To-morrow day I'll buy a spade,
When I'm out walking with the maid;
I tant put that here in my pottet!
But I can use it when I've dot it.
Here's some more sings in my pottet,
Here's my lead, and here's my string;
And once I had an iron ring,
But through a hole it lost one day,
And this is what I always say —
A hole's the worst sing in a pottet,
Be sure and mend it when you've dot it.

## GOOD ADVICE.

WHEN the cold wind blows,
　　Look out for your nose,
That it does not get froze;
And wrap up your toes
In warm woollen hose.
Now this I suppose
Was first written in prose,
By some one, who knows
The effects of cold snows.

———◆———

## LITTLE FLORA.

LITTLE Flora is three years old,
　　With clustering ringlets of fine, bright gold;
For a grown-up lady she's rather small,
　　But still she wanted a water-fall.

So Auntie twisted the silky red
　　In a little knot at the back of her head;
No lady in all the country wide,
　　Could look more sweet or dignified.

What a baby-matron the darling is!
　　What a soft, soft cheek to pat and kiss!
What a sparkling eye to play at care!
　　What a sober look the dimples wear!

Yet the only thing the least bit old,
 Is that little twist of sunny gold,
And the baby with her water-fall,
 Is only a baby — after all.

The Nursery.

———

## TWENTY FROGGIES.

TWENTY froggies went to school
 Down beside a rushing pool.
Twenty little coats of green,
 Twenty vests all white and clean.

"We must be in time," said they,
 First we study, then we play;"
That is how we keep the rule,
 When we froggies go to school.

Master Bull-frog, brave and stern,
 Called his classes in their turn,
Taught them how to nobly strive,
 Also how to leap and dive.

Taught them how to dodge a blow,
 From the sticks that bad boys throw;
Twenty froggies grew up fast,
 Bull-frogs they became at last.

Polished in a high degree,
 As each froggie ought to be,
Now they sit on other logs,
 Teaching other little frogs.

GEORGE COOPER.

## SUSIE MILLER.

SUSIE Miller burnt her little finger,
 Susie Miller burnt her little finger,
Susie Miller burnt her little finger,
One little finger burnt.
One little, two little, three little fingers,
Four little, five little, six little fingers,
Seven little, eight little, nine little fingers,
Ten little fingers burnt.

---

## WATCHING FOR PA!

THREE little forms in the twilight gray
 Scanning the shadows across the way;
Two pair of black eyes, and one of blue,—
Brimful of love, and of mischief, too,—
  Watching for Pa!
  Watching for Pa!
  Sitting by the window,
  Watching for Pa!

May, with her placid and thoughtful brow,
Gleaming with kindness and love just now;
Willie, the youngest, so roguish and gay,
Stealing sly kisses from sister May, —
  Watching for Pa!
  Watching for Pa!
  Sitting by the window,
  Watching for Pa!

Nellie, with ringlets of sunny hue,
Cosily nestled between the two ;
Pressing her cheek to the window pane,
Wishing the absent one home again, —
 Watching for Pa !
 Watching for Pa !
 Sitting by the window,
 Watching for Pa !


Now there are shouts from the window seat,
There is a patter of childish feet ;
Gayly they rush thro' the lighted hall,
"Coming at last" is the joyful call, —
 Welcoming Pa !
 Welcoming Pa !
 Standing on the doorstep,
 Welcoming Pa !


## THE BABY.

WHAT is the sweetest thing below
 The overarching heavenly bow,
The greatest nuisance that you know ?
  The baby.


Who has a precious little nose,
And chubby limbs, and pinkish toes ?
Who kicks and tumbles, laughs and crows ?
  The baby.

On whom does mother kisses press?
Who in the night screams in distress?
Who in the morning screams no less?
> The baby.

Who never has a word to say,
But always has his own sweet way?
May heaven prolong his earthly stay —
> The baby.

———◆———

# WHERE DID YOU COME FROM, BABY DEAR?

WHERE did you come from, baby dear?
  Out of the everywhere into here.

Where did you get your eyes so blue?
Out of the sky, as I came through.

What makes the light in them sparkle and spin?
Some of the starry spikes left in.

Where did you get that little tear?
I found it waiting when I got here.

What makes your forehead so smooth and high?
A soft hand stroked it as I passed by.

What makes your cheek like a warm white rose?
I saw something better than anyone knows.

Whence that three-cornered smile of bliss?
Three angels gave me at once a kiss.

Where did you get this pretty ear?
God spoke, and it came out to hear.

Where did you get those arms and hands?
Love made itself into hooks and bands.

Feet, whence did you come, you darling things?
From the same box as the cherub's wings.

How did they all come just to be you?
God thought of me, and so I grew.

But how did you come to us, you dear?
God thought about you, and so I am here.

GEORGE MacDONALD.

---

## THE OWL AND THE PUSSY-CAT.

THE owl and the pussy-cat went to sea,
   In a beautiful pea-green boat,
They took some honey, and lots of money,
Wrapped up in a five-pound note.
The owl looked up to the moon above,
And sang to his light guitar,
"Oh, pussy, oh, pussy, oh, pussy, my love,
What a beautiful pussy you are, you are,
What a beautiful pussy you are.
Pussy said to the owl, "You beautiful fowl,
How charmingly sweet you sing,
Come let us be married, too long have we tarried,
But what shall we do for a ring?

So they sailed away for a year and a day,
To the land where the song-tree grows;
And there in a wood a piggy-wig stood,
With a ring in the end of his nose, his nose,
With a ring in the end of his nose.
"Dear pig, are you willing to sell for one shilling your
     ring?"
Says the piggy, "I will,"
So they took it away, and were married next day,
By the turkey who lives on the hill.
They dined upon mince, and slices of quince,
Which they ate with a runcible spoon;
And, hand in hand on the golden sand,
They danced by the light of the moon, the moon,
They danced by the light of the moon.

EDWARD LEAR.

---

## TOTTY'S ARITHMETIC.

ONE little head, worth its whole weight in gold,
    Over and over, a million times told.

Two shining eyes, full of innocent glee,
Brighter than diamonds ever could be.

Three pretty dimples, for fun to slip in,
Two in the cheeks, and one in the chin.

Four little fingers on each baby hand,
Fit for a princess of sweet Fairy-land.

Five on each hand, if we reckon Tom Thumb
Standing beside them, so stiff and so glum!

Six pearly teeth just within her red lips,
Over which merriment ripples and trips.

Seven bright ringlets, as yellow as gold,
Seeming the sunshine to gather and hold.

Eight tiny waves running over her hair,
Sunshine and shadow, they love to be there.

Nine precious words that Totty can say,
But she will learn new ones every day.

Ten little chubby, comical toes;
And that is as far as this lesson goes.

ELIZABETH STUART PHELPS IN *St. Nicholas.*

———◆———

## ROBIN REDBREAST.

PRETTY Robin Redbreast,
    Let me see inside your nest; —
Oh! the eggs — one — two — three —
    Just as sweet as sweet can be.

I won't touch them; never fear —
    I won't let my breath come near —
If I did you'd leave your nest,
    Naughty Robin Redbreast.

E. A. MATHERS IN *Our Little Ones.*

## LITTLE KITTY.

ONCE there was a little kitty,
  Whiter than snow;
In the barn she used to frolic,
  Long time ago.

In the barn a little mousie
  Ran to and fro;
For she heard the kitty coming,
  Long time ago.

Two eyes had little kitty,
  Black as a sloe;
And they spied the little mousie,
  Long time ago.

Four paws had little kitty,
  Paws soft as dough;
And they caught the little mousie,
  Long time ago.

Nine teeth had little kitty
  All in a row;
And they bit the little mousie,
  Long time ago.

When the teeth bit little mousie,
  Little mouse cried, "Oh!"
But she got away from kitty,
  Long time ago.

Kitty White so shyly comes,
  To catch the mousie Grey;
But mousie hears her softly step,
  And quickly runs away.

E. Prentiss.

---

## TOO FOGGY.

TWO little birds started out to sing
  When foggy was the weather,
They cleared their throats, and whetted their bills,
  And coughed and wheezed together.
They wheezed and coughed as hard as they could,
  In this dreadful foggy weather,
Till they spoiled their notes, and split their throats,
  And turned up their toes together.

---

## PINKETY-WINKETY-WEE.

PINKETY-winkety-wee!
  Ten pink fingers has she,
Ten pink toes,
One pink nose,
  And two eyes that can hardly see,
And they blink and blink, and they wink and wink,
So you can't tell whether they are blue or pink.

Pinkety-blinkety-winkety!
Not much hair on her head has she;
She has no teeth, and she cannot talk;
She is not strong enough yet to walk;

She cannot even so much as creep;
Most of the time she is fast asleep;
Whenever you ask her how she feels,
She only doubles her fist and squeals.
The queerest bundle you ever did see,
Is little Pinkety-winkety-wee.

———◆———

## THE THREE LITTLE BUGS.

THREE little bugs in a basket,
   And hardly room for two,
And one was yellow, and one was black,
   And one like me, or you —
The space was small, no doubt, for all,
But what should three bugs do?

Three little bugs in a basket,
   And hardly crumbs for two,
And all were selfish in their hearts,
   The same as I or you,
So the strong ones said, "We'll eat the crumbs,
And that's what we will do."

Three little bugs in a basket,
   And the beds but two would hold;
So they all three fell to quarrelling,
   The white, the black, and the gold,
And two of the bugs got under the rugs,
And one was out in the cold!

So he that was left in the basket,
Without a crumb to chew,
Or a thread to wrap himself withal,
When the winds across him blew,
Pulled one of the rugs from off the bugs,
And so the quarrel grew.

And so there were none in the basket —
Ah, pity 't is, 't is true !
But he that was frozen and starved, at last
A strength from his weakness drew,
And pulled the rugs from both the bugs,
And killed and ate them too.

Now when bugs live in a basket,
Though more than it can hold,
It seems to me they had better agree,
The white, the black, and the gold,
And share what comes of beds and crumbs,
And leave no bug in the cold.

——◆——

## ELEVEN LITTLE PUSSY-CATS.

ELEVEN little pussy-cats invited out to tea,
  Eleven cups of milk they had, as sweet as milk could
      be,
Eleven little silver spoons, to stir the sugar in,
Eleven little napkins white, each tucked beneath a chin.
Eleven little meows they gave, eleven little purrs,
Eleven little sneezes, too, though wrapped up in their furs.

Eleven times they washed their paws, when all the milk
was out ;
Eleven times they bobbed their heads, and said it was, no
doubt ;
Eleven times they thought they heard the squeaking of a
mouse ;
Eleven times they curtsied to the lady of the house ;
Eleven times they promised to drive away the thieves,
That picked the grapes upon the vines, and hid among the
leaves.
They kept their word, and one day shook eleven bunches
down,
To this same girl of 'leven years, who caught them in her
gown.

## DOLLIE'S DOCTOR.

"COME and see my dolly dear,
    Doctor, she is ill, I fear ;
Yesterday, do what I would,
She would taste no kind of food ;

"And she tosses, moans, and cries,
Doctor what would you advise ? "
" Hum ! ha ! good madam, tell me, pray,
What have you offered her to-day ?

"Ah ! yes, I see, a piece of cake,
The worst thing you could make her take ;
Ah, let me taste,— yes, yes, I fear
Too many plums and currants here.

"But stop, I must just taste again,
For that will make the matter plain."
"But doctor, so much pains you take,
I see you've eaten all the cake.

"I thank you kindly for your care,
But surely, that was hardly fair."
"Ah, dear me, did I eat the cake?
Well, it was for dear baby's sake.

"But keep her in her bed quite warm,
And you will see she'll take no harm;
At night and morning use once more
Her draught and powder as before.

"And she must not be over-fed,
But she may have a piece of bread;
To-morrow then I dare to say
She'll be quite well, good-day, good-day."

—◆—

## A DOLL'S WEDDING.

SAYS Ivanhoe to Mimi:
      "It is our wedding day;
And will you promise, dearest,
      Your husband to obey?"

And this is Mimi's answer:
      "With all my heart, my dear,
If you will never cause me
      To drop a single tear;

"If you will ask me nothing
    But what I want to do,
I 'll be a sweet, obedient,
    Delightful wife to you."

Says Mr. Fenwick, giving
    His brown mustache a twist:
" I shall command you, madam,
    To do whate'er I list!"

Miss Mimi answered, frowning,
    His very soul to freeze:
" Then, sir, I shall obey you
    Only just when I please!"

Says Ivanhoe to Mimi:
    "Let us to this agree,—
I will not speak one word to you,
    If you 'll not speak to me;

" Then we shall never quarrel,
    But through our dolly life
I 'll be a model husband,
    And you a model wife!"

And now all men and women,
    Who make them wedding calls,
Look on, and almost envy
    The bliss of these two dolls.

They seem so very smiling,—
    So graceful, kind, and bright!
And gaze upon each other
    Quite speechless with delight.

Never one cross word saying,
    They stand up side by side,
Patterns of good behavior,
    To every groom and bride.

Sweethearts, it is far better,—
    This truth they plainly teach,—
The solid gold of silence,
    Than the small change of speech!

LUCY LARCOM in St. Nicholas.

## NAUGHTY KITTY.

"OH! mother, you comb my hair in my eyes,"
    So peevish-tempered Miss Kitty cries.
"And you've hurt my ears so awful bad,
    I'll just scream and kick, I feel so mad!

"I hate to be washed, you know I do;
    And combing my hair puts me all in a stew;
You make the old soap go into my eye,
    And then you scold me because I cry.

"I wish I had never got out of bed;
    What do I care if I have a rough head?
And all soap and water I do despise;
    I think it was made to smart people's eyes."

"Why, Kitty!" her mother said, "I'm in fear
    That this naughty talk the neighbors should hear;
And then I don't know what I should do,
    I should feel so bad for myself and you."

"Well, I just don't care," naughty Kitty cried;
"No other girl ever was so much tried;
I don't care what they say about me or you."
And she cried out aloud, " Boo-oo, boo-oo!"

Oh! naughty Miss Kitty, indeed you're not pretty,
And you make my heart feel very sadly.
Little girls, all take warning, and watch every morning,
That *you* never behave so badly.

JULIA A. SHEARMAN.

## LITTLE MISS SNOWFLAKE.

LITTLE Miss Snowflake came to town
All dressed up in her brand-new gown,
And nobody looked as fresh and fair
As little Miss Snowflake, I declare!

Out of a fleecy cloud she stepped,
Where all the rest of her family kept
As close together as bees can swarm,
In readiness for a big snowstorm.

But little Miss Snowflake could n't wait,
And she wanted to come in greater state;
For she thought that her beauty would ne'er be known,
If she came in a crowd, so she came alone.

All alone from the great blue sky,
Where cloudy vessels went scudding by,
With sails all set, on their way to meet
The larger ships of the snowy fleet.

She was very tired, but could n't stop
On tall church spire, or chimney top;
All the way from her bright abode
Down to the dust. of a country road!

There she rested all out of breath,
And there she speedily met her death,
And nobody could exactly tell
The spot where little Miss Snowflake fell.

JOSEPHINE POLLARD.

## SATURDAY NIGHT.

PLACING the little hats all in a row;
     Ready for church on the morrow, you know;
Washing wee faces, and little black fists,
Getting them ready and fit to be kissed;
Putting them into clean garments and white;
That is what mothers are doing to-night.

Spying out holes in the little worn hose,
Laying by shoes that are worn thro' the toes,
Looking o'er garments so faded and thin —
Who but a mother knows where to begin?
Changing a button to make it look right —
That is what mothers are doing to-night.

Calling the little ones all round her chair,
Hearing them lisp forth their evening prayer,
Telling them stories of Jesus of old,
Who loves to gather the lambs to his fold;
Watching, they listen with childish delight —
That is what mothers are doing to-night.

Creeping so softly to take a last peep,
After the little ones all are asleep;
Anxious to know if the children are warm,
Tucking the blanket round each little form;
Kissing each little face, rosy and bright —
That is what mothers are doing to-night.

Kneeling down gently beside the white bed,
Lowly and meekly she bows down her head,
Praying as only a mother can pray,
"God guide and keep them from going astray."

## KEEPSAKES.

TWO little baby boys I own;
   The elder scarcely walks alone;
His sunny hair, and large brown eyes,
His earnest look of sweet surprise,
His funny ways, and joyous shout,
I could not tell all about,
     If I should try a year.

He creeps so fast to catch his toys,
And then he sets up such a noise;
His horse and dog, and book and bell,
He throws them all about, pell mell.
Oh, Mother Goose, if you could see
This little boy so full of glee,
     Your sides would ache, I fear.

He watches with a rueful face
The baby, who usurps his place.
My darling boy, your little nose
Had to be broken, I suppose.
'T is very odd sometimes the way
You love your " bubber " in your play,
　　　And bring a smile or tear.

In hammock low among the trees,
Rocked back and forth by passing breeze,
The baby swings, and coos to see
The gentle rustle of the tree.
The lights and shades, the leaves that fall,
The sunshine breeding over all —
　　　'T is Indian Summer here.

Way overhead, in the blue sky,
Downy clouds float softly by;
A lullaby fair nature sings,
And through the air its music rings;
My little one falls fast asleep,
As sun and shadow o'er him creep,
　　　His mother watching near.

Two baby boys! a God of love
Sends us a gift from heaven above;
And like the shifting rainbow bright,
Tinging and drifting clouds with light,
Their souls, so fine and sweet, shine out,
Breaking through mists of grief and doubt,
　　　And make my pathway clear.

## JESUS' NAME.

A LITTLE girl, with golden head,
    Asked me to read a minute,
"A pretty story," as she said,
    "For Jesus' name was in it."

The pleasant task was soon complete,
    But long I pondered of it,
That Jesus' name should be so sweet,
    That e'en a child should love it.

O, sweetest story ever told!
    What tongue would dare begin it,
If it were riven of its gold,
    And Jesus' name not in it?

S. B. LEVERICH.

---

## THE HOME OF THE ROBIN.

SAID little Cock Robin
    One bright day in March,
"Let's build our spring nest
    In this beautiful larch."

Said his dear little mate,
    "To this I agree,
I see nowhere around
    Such a suitable tree."

Said little Cock Robin,
　　"Now quickly we'll work,
I'll bring some fine twigs,
　　And these pieces of cork."

Said his dear little mate,
　　"Your work I admire,
To be your help-mate
　　I fondly aspire.

These pieces of cord
　　We'll weave around tight,
And fasten them firmly
　　Before it is night."

Then down in the meadow
　　They found some nice clay,
And plastered their walls,
　　On one fine sunny day.

Three bonny blue eggs
　　There soon do we see,
In this nest lined with down,
　　On a branch, in the tree.

The sun rose and set,
　　The days longer grew,
Peep! peep! cried the chicks,
　　From those bonny eggs blue.

As love ruled the parents,
　　So love ruled the three
Little soft downy nestlings,
　　In this noble larch tree.

Each took in its turn,
    From its dear parent's bill,
A fly, bug, or worm,
    Or little bread pill.

Said little Cock Robin,
    "Wherever I look,
I find nothing so nice
    As our own little nook."

Said his sweet little mate,
    "To this I agree,"
So love and content
    Ruled this home in the tree.

                    JENNY WALLIS.

———————

## CHARLEY AND HIS KITTY.

"WHERE is my little basket gone?"
    Said Charley boy, one day.
"I guess some little boy or girl
    Has taken it away."

"And kitty too, I can't find her,
    Oh dear, what shall I do!
I wish I could my basket find,
    And little kitty too.

"I'll run to mamma's room, and look,
    Perhaps she may be there,
For kitty loves to take a nap
    In mamma's easy chair.

Oh, mamma, mamma, come and look,
    See what a little heap,
My kitty's in the basket here,
    All cuddled down to sleep."

He took it very carefully,
    And carried it in a minute,
And showed it to his mamma dear,
    With little kitty in it.
                    Eliza Follen.

## THE DEAD DOLL.

YOU need n't be trying to comfort me — I tell you my
    dolly is dead!
There is no use in saying she is n't, with a crack like that
    in her head.
It's just like you said it would n't hurt much to have my
    tooth out, that day;
And then, when the man 'most pulled my head off, you
    had n't a word to say.

And I guess you must think I'm a baby, when you say
    you can mend it with glue!
As if I did n't know better than that! Why, just suppose
    it was you?
You might make her look all mended — but what do I
    care for looks?
Why, glue's for chairs and tables, and toys, and the backs
    of books!

My dolly! my own little daughter! Oh, but it's the awful-
    est crack!
It just makes me sick to think of the sound, when her
    poor head went whack
Against that horrible brass thing, that holds up the little
    shelf.
Now, Nursey, what makes you remind me? I know that
    I did it myself!

I think you must be crazy — you'll get her another head!
What good would forty heads do her? I tell you my dolly
    is dead!
And to think I hadn't quite finished her elegant new
    spring hat!
And I took a sweet ribbon of hers last night, to tie on
    that horrid cat!

When my mamma gave me that ribbon — I was playing
    out in the yard —
She said to me most expressly, "Here's a ribbon for Hilde-
    garde,"
And I went and put it on Tabby, and Hildegarde saw me
    do it;
But I said to myself, "Oh, never mind, I don't believe
    she knew it?"

But I know that she knew it now, and I just believe, I
    do,
That her poor little heart was broken, and so her head
    broke too.
Oh, my baby, my little baby! I wish my head had been
    hit!
For I've hit it over and over, and it hasn't cracked a bit.

But since the darling is dead, she'll want to be buried, of
　　course ;
We will take my little wagon, Nurse, and you shall be
　　the horse,
And I'll walk behind and cry ; and we'll put her in this,
　　you see —
This dear little box — and we'll bury her then under the
　　maple tree.

And papa will make me a tombstone, like the one he made
　　for my bird ;
And he'll put what I tell him on it — yes, every single
　　word !
I shall say : — "Here lies Hildegarde, a beautiful doll who is
　　dead ;
She died of a broken heart, and a dreadful crack in her
　　head."

Margaret Vandegrift in St. Nicholas.

## THE SMILING DOLLY.

I WHISPERED to my dolly,
　　And told her not to tell,
(She's a really lovely dolly —
　　Her name is Rosabel).

"Rosy," I said, "stop smiling,
　　For I've been dreadful bad !
You mustn't look so pleasant,
　　As if you feel real glad !

"I took mamma's new ear-ring —
  I did, now, Rosabel —
And I never even asked her —
  Now, Rosy, don't you tell!

"You see I'll try to find it
  Before I let her know;
She'd feel so very sorry
  To think I'd acted so."

I had wheeled her round the garden
  In her gig till I was lame;
Yet when I told my trouble,
  She smiled on just the same!

Her hair waved down her shoulders
  Like silk, all made of gold.
I kissed her, then I shook her,
  Oh, dear! how I did scold!

"You're really naughty, Rosy,
  To look so when I cry.
When my mamma's in trouble
  I never laugh — not I."

And still she kept on smiling,
  The queer, provoking child!
I shook her well, and told her
  Her conduct drove me wild.

When — only think! that ear-ring
  Fell out of Rosy's hair!
When I had dressed the darling,
  I must have dropped it there.

She doubled when I saw it,
　And almost hit her head;
Again I whispered softly,
　And this is what I said:

"You precious, precious Rosy!
　Now I'll go tell mamma
How bad I was — and sorry —
　And, O, how good you are!

"For, Rose, I had n't lost it;
　You knew it all the while,
You knew I'd shake it out, dear,
　And that's what made you smile."

　　　　　MARY MAPES DODGE in *St. Nicholas.*

———◆———

## ALL THE CHILDREN.

I SUPPOSE if all the children
　Who have lived through the ages long,
Were collected and inspected,
　They would make a wondrous throng.
Oh! the babble of the Babel!
　Oh, the flutter and the fuss!
To begin with Cain and Abel,
　And to finish up with us.

Think of all the men and women
　Who are now, and who have been —
Every nation since creation,
　That this world of ours has seen.

And of all of them, not any
    But was once a baby small;
While of children, oh, how many
    Have not grown up at all!

Some have never laughed or spoken,
    Never used their rosy feet;
Some have even flown to heaven
    Ere they knew that earth was sweet;
And, indeed, I wonder whether,
    If we reckon every birth,
And bring such a flock together,
    There is room for them on earth.

Who will wash their smiling faces?
    Who their saucy ears will box?
Who will dress them and caress them?
    Who will darn their little socks?
Where are arms enough to hold them?
    Hands to pat each shining head?
Who will praise them? Who will scold them?
    Who will pack them off to bed?

Little happy Christian children,
    Little savage children, too,
In all stages, of all ages
    That our planet ever knew —
Little princes and princesses,
    Little beggers wan and faint:
Some in very handsome dresses,
    Naked some, bedaubed with paint.

Only think of the confusion
　　Such a motley crowd would make,
And the clatter of their chatter,
　　And the things that they would break!
Oh, the babble of the Babel!
　　Oh, the flutter and the fuss!
To begin with Cain and Abel,
　　And to finish up with us.

*The Welcome.*

## A MOTHER'S DIARY.

MORNING!—Baby on the floor,
　　Making for the fender;
Sunlight seems to make him sneeze,
　　Baby "on the bender;"
All the spools upset and gone,
　　Chairs drawn into file,
Harnessed strings all strung across,
　　Ought to make one smile.
Apron clean, curls smooth, eyes blue,
　　(How these charms will dwindle!)
For I rather think, don't you?
　　Baby is "a swindle."

Noon!—A tangled silken floss,
　　Getting in blue eyes,
Apron that will not keep clean;
　　If a baby tries!
One blue shoe untied, and one
　　Underneath the table;
Chairs gone mad, and blocks and toys,
　　Well as they are able,

Baby in a high chair, too,
  Yelling for his dinner.
Spoon in mouth; I think, don't you?
  Baby is a sinner.

Night! — Chairs all set back again,
  Blocks and spools in order.
One blue shoe beneath the mat,
  Tells of the maurauder.
Apron folded on a chair,
  Plaid dress torn and wrinkled;
Two pink feet kicked pretty bare,
  Little fat knees crinkled;
In his crib, and conquered, too,
  By sleep, blest evangel;
Now, I surely think, don't you?
  Baby is an angel!

BERTHA SCRANTON POOL.

## WILLIE'S QUESTION.

WILLIE sat and watched his grandpa
    When he came to visit him,
With his spectacles a-glisten,
    O'er the eyes with age grown dim;
And the child-eyes filled with wonder,
    And a sense of envy rose,
When he took them off to wipe them,
    And replaced them on his nose.

When his grandpa's visit ended,
    Willie sought for some advice.
"Papa," said he " can I ever
    Do like grandpa with my eyes?
Can I string 'em, just like grandpa,
    On a wire — and when I cough,
Just like grandpa did, you 'member,
    Can I take my two eyes off?"

EBEN E. REXFORD.

## LEARNING TO PRAY.

KNEELING, fair in the twilight gray,
    A beautiful child was trying to pray;
His cheek on his mother's knee,
    His bare little feet half hidden,
    His smile still coming unbidden,
And his heart brimful of glee.

"I want to laugh.  Is it naughty?  Say,
O mamma! I 've had such fun to-day,
    I hardly can say my prayers.
    I don't feel just like praying;
    I want to be out-doors playing,
And run, all undressed, down stairs.

" I can see the flowers in the garden bed,
Shining so pretty and sweet and red :
    And Sammy is swinging, I guess.
    Oh! everything is so fine out there,
    I want to put it all in the prayer.
(Do you mean I can do it by 'Yes'?)

"When I say, 'Now I lay me'—word for word—
It seems to me as if nobody heard.
  Would 'Thank you, dear God,' be right?
    He gave me my mammy,
    And papa, and Sammy—
  O mamma! you nodded I might."

Clasping his hands, and hiding his face,
Unconsciously yearning for help and grace,
  The little one now began.
    His mother's nod, and sanction sweet,
    Had led him close to the dear Lord's feet,
  And his words like music ran.

"Thank you for making this home so nice,
The flowers, and folks, and my two white mice.
  (I wish I could keep right on.)
    I thank you, too, for every day—
    Only I'm most too glad to pray.
  Dear God, I think I am done.

"Now, mamma, rock me—just a minute—
And sing the hymn with 'darling' in it.
  I wish I could say my prayers!
    When I get big I know I can.
    Oh! won't it be nice to be a man,
  And stay all night down stairs!"

The mother, singing, clasped him tight,
Kissing and cooing her fond "Good-night"
  And treasured his every word.
    For well she knew that the artless joy
    And love of her precious, innocent boy,
  Were a prayer that her Lord had heard.

MARY MAPES DODGE.

## PLAY.

PLAY you were a princess,
  And this was your diamond throne
Play I was a fairy —
  " That is the truth, my own ! "

Play you were a giant,
  And I was a poor lost girl ;
Play this was your castle ;
" Think I could harm one curl ? "

Play this was my carriage,
  And I was a lady grand ;
Play that was a ball room :
  " Lady, I kiss your hand ! "

Play the sun was a kite,
  And this was the yellow string ;
Play I was a robin ;
  " Sing, little birdie, sing ? "

Play you were a shepherd,
  And searching with weary feet ;
Play I was your lambkin ;
  " Come to your fold, my sweet ! "

Soon eyelids are drooping,
  And that was a sigh, so deep ;
Play this was the night, ma :
  And play I had gone to sleep !

GEORGE COOPER.

## WHERE SHALL BABY'S DIMPLE BE?

OVER the cradle a mother hung,
    Softly crooning a slumber song,
And these were the simple words she sung
    All the evening long:

"Cheek or chin, or knuckle or knee,
Where shall the baby's dimple be?
Where shall the angel's finger rest
When he comes down to the baby's nest?
Where shall the angel's touch remain
When he awakens my babe again?"

Still as she bent and sang so low,
    A murmur into her music broke,
And she paused to hear, for she could but know
    The baby's angel spoke:

"Cheek or chin, or knuckle or knee,
Where shall the baby's dimple be?
Where shall my finger fall and rest
When I come down to the baby's nest?
Where shall my finger's touch remain
When I awaken your babe again?"

Silent the mother sat, and dwelt
    Long on the sweet delay of choice,
And then by her baby's side she knelt,
    And sang with pleasant voice:

"Not on the limb, O angel dear!
For the charms with its youth will disappear;
Not on the check shall the dimple be,
For the harboring smile will fade and flee;
But touch thou the chin with an impress deep,
And my baby the angel's seal shall keep."

DR. J. G. HOLLAND in *Hours at Home.*

---

## THE SUNDAY BABY.

YOU wonderful little Sunday child!
   Half of your fortune scarce you know,
Although you have blinked and winked and smiled
   Full seven and twenty days below.

"The bairn that is born on a Sabbath day"—
   So say the old wives over their glass—
"Is bonny and healthy, and wise and gay!"
   What do you think of that, my lass?

Health and wisdom, and beauty and mirth!
   And (as if that were not enough for a dower),
Because of the holy day of your birth,
   Abroad you may walk in the gloaming's hour.

When we poor bodies, with backward look,
   Shiver and quiver and shake, with fear
Of fiend and fairy, and kelpie and spook,
   Never a thought need you take, my dear—

For "Sunday's child" may go where it please,
   Sunday's child shall be free from harm!
Right down through the mountain-side it sees
   The mines unopened where jewels swarm!

O fortunate baby! Sunday lass!
  The veins of gold through the rocks you'll see;
And when o'er the shining sands you pass,
  You can tell where the hidden springs may be.

And never a fiend, or an airy sprite
  May thwart or hinder you all your days;
Whenever it chances in mirk midnight,
  The lids of your marvellous eyes you raise.

You may see, while your heart is pure and true,
  The angels, that visit this lower sphere,
Drop down the firmament, two and two,
  Their errands of mercy to work down here.

This is the dower of a Sunday child;
  What do you think of it, little brown head,
Winking and blinking your eyes so mild,
  Down in the depth of your snowy bed?

ALICE WILLIAMS in *St. Nicholas.*

## MINNIE AND WINNIE.

MINNIE and Winnie
    Slept in a shell.
Sleep, little ladies!
    And they slept well.

Pink was the shell within,
    Silver without;
Sounds of the great sea
    Wander'd about.

Sleep little ladies!
 Wake not soon!
Echo on echo
 Dies to the moon.

Two bright stars
 Peep'd into the shell.
"What are they dreaming of?
 Who can tell?"

Started a green linnet
 Out of the croft;
Wake, little ladies,
 The sun is aloft!

Alfred Tennyson in St. Nicholas.

## GOOD FOR SOMETHING.

"DOOD-FOR-NOSSIN 'ittle son,
 Papa tells me, jes for fun,
I duess — fer, ma, oo say
I dood for sumsin all ee day."
And so you are, my precious one,
Full of mischief, love, and fun;
Good to fill our hearts with joy,
Our darling blue-eyed little boy!
Good to clutter up the room;
Good to ride astride the broom;
Good to tip my basket o'er,
Rolling spools about the floor;
Good to pull the baby's hair,
And make a horse of every chair;

Good to tumble on the floor,
And shut poor fingers in the door;
Good to wear out little shoes,
And mamma's wax and thimble lose,
Good "dear danpa's" specs to hide,
And on his foot to "take a yide;"
Good, when let out doors to play,
To ope the gate and run away;
Good to watch for "papa tum,"
And clap wee hands when he gets home;
Good to climb up on his knee,
And laugh and shout with boyish glee;
Good, when wearied out with play,
Your head on mamma's lap to lay,
Quite ready now to be undressed,
And in her arms be lulled to rest
By stories, which you like so well,
Of "Jack and Jill," and "Ding-dong bell;"
Good, ere cuddling down to sleep,
To pray the Lord your soul to keep;
Good to wake up with the day,
And fold your little hands and say:
"Dear Dod, do bess my dear mamma,
My baby sister, and papa,
And 'ittle Willie, too, I pway,
And teep us safe froo-out ee day."
Ah! good for many things thou art,
Our bonny boy with blithesome heart,
Our boy with many a winsome way,
Mishap and prank and merry play;
Our "dood-for-nossin 'ittle son."
As papa call you, "jes for fun."

# THE NEW DOLL.

YOU 'RE a beautiful, beautiful dolly,
 And dressed like a sweet little queen
Not to care for you, dear, may seem folly,
 When I 've but a rag-doll so mean.
I know that its arms are the queerest ;
 Its head very funny and flat ;
Its eyes anything but the clearest ;
 Yet old friends are best, for all that.

Your hair falls in ringlets so flaxen,
 Your eyes are delightfully blue,
Your cheeks they are rosy and waxen,
 You 're charming, I 'll give you your due.
Yet shall I give up Betsy Baker,
 Who has n't a shoe nor a hat,
Because you 've a splendid dress-maker ?
 No ! old friends are best, for all that.

You came Christmas morn in my stocking ;
 I ought to be proud, I suppose,
And not to be pleased would be shocking :
 Do, Betsy dear, turn out your toes.
Oh, you are my every-day dolly !
 And this one in silk dress and hat
I 'll put on the shelf ; call it folly,
 Yet old friends are best, for all that.

## CHILD-SONG.

### THE CITY CHILD.

DAINTY little maiden, whither would you wander?
   Whither from this pretty home, the home where
      mother dwells?
"Far and far away," said the dainty little maiden,
"All among the gardens, auriculas, anemones,
Roses and lilies, and Canterbury-bells." ·

Dainty little maiden, whither would you wander?
Whither from this pretty house, this city house of ours?
"Far and far away," said the dainty little maiden,
"All among the meadows, the clover and the clematis,
Daisies and kingcups, and honeysuckle flowers."

ALFRED TENNYSON in St. Nicholas.

## COMING.

BEAUTIFUL things there are coming this way,
   Nearer and nearer, dear, every day —
      Yes, closer and closer, my baby.

Mischievous showers, and faint little smells
Of far-away flowers in far-away dells,
      Are coming in April, my baby.

Sly little blossoms that clamber along,
Close to the ground, till they grow big and strong,
      Are coming in May, little baby.

Roses and bees, and a big, yellow moon,
Coming together in beautiful June,
     In lovely midsummer, my baby.

Pretty red cherries, and bright little flies,
Twinkling and turning the fields into skies,
     Will come in July, little baby.

Feathery clouds, and long afternoons,
Scarce a leaf stirring, and birdie's soft croons,
     Are coming in August, my baby.

Glimpses of blue through the poppies and wheat,
And one little birthday, with swift-flying feet,
     Will come in September, my baby.

LAURA LEDYARD.

## PITTY PAT'S PRAYER.

WE'VE a dear little lassie we've named Pitty Pat,
     She's got a wee kitten she calls Kitty Cat;
Now Pitty Pat sleeps in a gown snowy white,
While Kitty Cat wears her day clothing all night.

But Pitty Pat says she don't like it at all,
And, pulling the fur out, makes Kitty Cat squall;
But still she persists in undressing her pet,
And failing to do it, quite angry will get.

While Kitty Cat cries at what Pitty Pat does
To her one little coatee of silky soft fuz,
Then Pitty Pat's sorry, and asks why she cries
At being fixed tidy for shutting her eyes.

Nor says "Now I lay me," when going to bed,
But, curling up, softly sings "purr" instead.
So Pitty Pat tells her, in solemnest way,
"If you 're a bad Kitty Cat, then I must pray."

"Her lays her — dear Father — down softly — in bed —
Her does n't — do nuffin — and nuffin — her said —
'Cept pur-r — and pur-r — and then goes to sleep —
But never mind, Father, her little soul keep!"

———◆———

## LITTLE TEASE.

HIDING her grandmamma's knitting away,
 Teaching the kittens their letters, in play,
Clambering up to the table or shelf,
Having a tea-party all by herself.
Quiet a minute, in mischief, no doubt,
Pulling the needles and thimbles about.
Sewing her apron, demure as you please;
Anyone got such a dear little tease?

Printing her hands in the soft, tempting flour,
Tumbles and bumps twenty times in an hour;
Tangling the yarn, and unravelling the lace,
Doing it all with the prettiest grace.
Mother is scolding her very bad girl,
Says she sets the whole house in a whirl!
Looks at her pouting there down by her knees,
Clasps to her heart again, dear little tease.

*Little Corporal.*

## GRAN'MA AL'AS DOES.

I WANTS to mend my wagon,
  And has to have some nails;
Jus' two, free will be plenty,
  We're going to haul our rails.
The splendidest cob fences
  We're making ever was!
I wis' you'd help us find 'em,
  Gran'ma al'as does.


My horse's name is Betsy;
  She jumped and broke her head;
I put her in the stable,
  And fed her on milk and bread.
The stable's in the parlor;
  We didn't make no muss;
I wis' you'd let it stay there,
  Gran'ma al'as does.


I's going to the corn-fields,
  To ride on Charlie's plow;
I spect he'd like to have me;
  I wants to go right now.
Oh, won't I gee-up awful,
  And whoa like Charlie whoas;
I wis' you wouldn't bozzer,
  Gran'ma never does.

I want some bread and butter;
  I's hungry worstest kind;
But Taddie must n't have none,
  'Cause she would n't mind.
Put plenty sugar on it;
  I tell you what I knows,
It's *right* to put on sugar,
  Gran'ma al'as does.

A. H. Poe.

## THE FOOLISH ROBIN.

O SWEET little girl, 'neath the white blossoms sitting,
  Watching the robins through the apple-trees flitting,
Straw hat trimmed with flowers, and eyes of true blue,
Now tell me the story the robin told you.

And this is the story, as told by the robin
To Blue-eyes, who answered him only by sobbing,
For who, as he listens to robin's sad fate,
Could refrain from lamenting with him his dear mate.

"My mate, Madam Redbreast, said, 'Hurry up, Bob,
I must have a warm nest that the boys cannot rob,
I have three little eggs all speckled with blue,
If you'll build me a nest I will hatch them for you.'

"I flew about quickly, worked early and late,
I finished the nest, and called my dear mate,
'Oh Robin,' said she, 'what have you been about?
You've built this nice nest in the old eaves' spout.

"'The rain it will drown both your birdies and me,
You'd better have built in the old apple-tree.'
But she laid down her eggs, and hatched them out there,
Little Bob, Dickey Red-Breast, and Yellow-bill fair.

"Alas, for my mate, and my little birds three !
I wish, oh, I wish I had built in the tree !
My poor little birds were all washed out and drowned,
And I found my dear mate lying dead on the ground."

*Churchman.*

## WHAT ROBIN TOLD.

HOW do the robins build their nest ?
    Robin Redbreast told me.
First a wisp of amber hay
In a pretty round they lay,
Then some shreds of downy floss,
Feathers, too, and bits of moss,
Woven with a sweet, sweet song,
This way, that way, and across ;
    That's what Robin told me.

Where do the robins hide their nests ?
    Robin Redbreast told me.
Up among the leaves so deep,
Where the sunbeams rarely creep ;
Long before the winds are cold,
Long before the leaves are gold,
Bright-eyed stars will peep, and see
Baby robins, one, two, three ;
    That's what Robin told me.

GEO. COOPER.

# THE FIRST PARTY.

MISS Anabel McCarty was invited to a party,
　　"Your company from six to ten," the invitation said,
And the maiden was delighted, to think she was invited
To sit up till the hour when the big folks went to bed.

The crazy little midget ran and told the news to Bridget,
Who clapped her hands, and danced a jig to Anabel's de-
　　　　light,
And said with accents hearty, "'Twill be the swatest
　　　　party,
If you're there yourself, my darlint, and I wish it were
　　　　to-night."

The great amount of frilling was positively killing,
And oh, the little booties, and the lovely sash so wide,
And the gloves so very cunning, she was altogether stun-
　　　　ning,
And the whole McCarty family regarded her with pride.

They gave minute directions, with copious interjections,
As, "Sit up straight," and "Don't do this or that,
　　　　't would be absurd."
But what with their caressing, and the agony of dressing,
Miss Anabel McCarty did not hear a single word.

There was music, there was dancing, and the sight was
　　　　most entrancing,
As if fairy-land and flora-land were holding jubilee ;

There was laughing, there was shouting, there was crying,
  there was pouting,
And old and young together made a carnival of glee.

The noise kept growing louder, and the naughty boys
  would crowd her,
"I think you're very rude indeed," the little maiden said,
And then without a warning, her whole instruction scorn-
  ing,
She screamed, "I want my supper, and I want to go to
  bed."

Now big folks, who are older, do not laugh at her or scold
  her,
For if the simple truth were told, you 've often felt inclined
To leave a ball or party, as did Anabel McCarty,
But you had n't half her courage, and you could n't speak
  your mind.

---

## LITTLE MOLLY.

WHAT will the dear St. Nicholas bring
    For a little girl like me?
Will he fill my stocking with picture books,
    Pretty as pretty can be?

Will he bring me a doll with "truly hair,"
    And cheeks a lovely red?
Will he bring me — Oh, if he only would —
    A dear little trundle bed?

Will he bring me cups, and saucers, and spoons?
　　Oh dear, how glad I'd be!
And a little tea-pot, and tea-kettle,
　　That I can play make tea!

Do you think he can quite afford so much,
　　For a little girl like me?
If he only could, and would give them all,
　　What a happy girl I'd be!

C. A. S.

---

## BABY FINGERS.

TEN little fat fingers so taper and neat;
　　Ten fat little fingers so rosy and sweet!
Eagerly reaching for all that comes near,
Now poking your eyes out, and pulling your hair,
Soothing and patting with velvet-like touch,
Then digging your cheek with a mischievous clutch;
Gently waving good-by with infantile grace,
Then dragging your bonnet down over your face.
Beating pat-a-cake, pat-a-cake, slow and sedate,
Then tearing your book at a furious rate;
Gravely holding them out, like a king, to be kissed,
Then thumping the window with tightly-closed fist;
Now lying asleep, all dimpled and warm,
On the white cradled pillow, secure from all harm.
O, dear baby hands! how much love you enfold
In the weak, careless clasp of those fingers' soft hold!
Keep spotless as now, through the world's evil ways,
And bless with fond care our last weariful days.

Mrs. RICHARD GRANT WHITE.

# NURSERY SONG.

AS I walked over the hill one day,
   I listened, and heard a mother-sheep say,
"In all the green world there is nothing so sweet
As my little lammie, with his nimble feet;
      With his eye so bright,
      And his wool so white,
Oh, he is my darling, my heart's delight!"
And the mother-sheep and her little one
Side by side lay down in the sun;
And they went to sleep on the hillside warm,
While my little lammie lies here on my arm.

I went to the kitchen, and what did I see,
But the old gray cat with her kittens three!
I heard her whispering soft; said she,
"My kittens, with tails so cunningly curled,
Are the prettiest things that can be in the world.
      The bird on the tree,
      And the old ewe, she,
   May love their babies exceedingly;
   But I love my kittens there,
   Under the rocking-chair.
I love my kittens with all my might,
I love them at morning, noon, and night.
Now I'll take up my kitties, the kitties I love,
And we'll lie down together beneath the warm stove."
Let the kittens sleep under the stove so warm,
While my little darling lies here on my arm.

I went to the yard, and I saw the old hen
Go clucking about, with her chickens ten ;
She clucked, and she scratched, and she bustled away,
And what do you think I heard the hen say ?
I heard her say, " The sun never did shine
On anything like to these chickens of mine.
You may hunt the full moon and the stars, if you please,
But you never will find ten such chickens as these.
My dear, downy darlings, my sweet little things,
Come, nestle now cozily under my wings."
So the hen said, and the chickens all sped,
As fast as they could, to their nice feather bed.
And there let them sleep, in their feathers so warm,
While my little chick lies here on my arm.

MRS. CARTER.

---

## THE CHANGELING.

### A STORY TOLD TO GRACIE.

ONE day in summer's glow,
  Not many years ago,
A little baby lay upon my knee,
  With rings of silken hair,
  And fingers waxen fair,
Tiny and soft, and pink as pink could be.

We watched it thrive and grow, —
  Ah me ! we loved it so, —
And marked its daily gain of sweeter charms ;
  It learned to laugh and crow,
  And play, and kiss us — so —
Until one day we missed it from our arms.

In sudden, strange surprise
We met each other's eyes,
Asking, "Who stole our pretty babe away?"
We questioned earth and air,
But, seeking everywhere,
We never found it from that summer day.

But in its wonted place
There was another face, —
A little girl's, with yellow curly hair
About her shoulders tossed,
And the sweet babe we lost
Seemed sometimes looking from her eyes so fair.

She dances, romps, and sings,
And does a hundred things
Which my lost baby never tried to do;
She longs to read in books,
And with bright, eager looks
Is always asking questions strange and new.

And I can scarcely tell,
I love the rogue so well,
Whether I would retrace the four years' track,
And lose the merry sprite,
Who makes my home so bright,
To have again my little baby back.

Ah, blue eyes! do you see
Who stole my babe from me,
And brought the little girl from fairy clime?
A gray old man with wings,
Who steals all precious things;
He lives forever, and his name is Time.

He rules the world, they say:
He took my babe away—
My precious babe—and left me in its place,
This little maiden fair,
With yellow curly hair,
Who lives on stories, and whose name is Grace!

ELISABETH AKERS ALLEN in *Our Young Folks.*

—◆—

## HANG UP THE BABY'S STOCKING.

HANG up the baby's stocking;
  Be sure you don't forget—
The dear little dimpled darling!
  She ne'er saw Christmas yet;
But I've told her all about it,
  And she opened her big blue eyes,
And I'm sure she understands it,
  She looked so funny and wise.

Dear! what a tiny stocking!
  It does n't take much to hold
Such little pink toes as baby's,
  Away from the frost and cold.
But then for the baby's Christmas
  It will never do at all;
Why, Santa would n't be looking
  For anything half so small!

I know what we 'll do for the baby—
  I 've thought of the very best plan—
I 'll borrow a stocking of grandma,
  The longest that ever I can;

And you'll hang it by mine, dear mother,
　　Right here in the corner, so,
And write a letter to Santa,
　　And fasten it on to the toe.

Write "This is the baby's stocking
　　That hangs in the corner here;
You never have seen her, Santa,
　　For she only came this year;
But she's just the blessedest baby —
　　And now, before you go,
Just cram her stocking with goodies,
　　From the top clean down to the toe."

*Little Corporal.*

## THE BABY I LOVE.

THIS is the baby I love!
　　The baby that cannot talk;
The baby that cannot walk;
The baby that just begins to creep;
The baby that's cuddled, and rocked to sleep;
　　Oh, this is the baby I love!

This is the baby I love!
The baby that's never cross;
The baby that papa can toss;
The baby that crows when held aloft;
The baby that's rosy, and round, and soft!
　　Oh, this is the baby I love!

This is the baby I love!
The baby that laughs when I peep
To see is it still asleep;

The baby that coos, and frowns, and blinks,
When left alone, as it sometimes *thinks;*
    Oh, this is the baby I love!

    This is the baby I love!
    The baby that lies on my knee,
    And dimples and smiles on me,
While I strip it, and bathe it, and kiss it, Oh!
Till with bathing and kissing 't is all aglow;
    Yes, this is the baby I love!

    This is the baby I love!
    The baby all freshly dressed;
    That waking is never at rest;
That plucks at my collar, and pulls my hair,
Till I look like a witch, but I do not care;
    Oh, this is the baby I love!

    This is the baby I love!
    The baby that understands,
    And dances with feet and hands,
And a sweet little whinnying, eager cry
For the nice warm breakfast that waits it close by;
    Oh, this is the baby I love!

    This is the baby I love!
    The baby that tries to talk;
    The baby that longs to walk;
And Oh! its mamma will wake some day,
To find that her baby has *run away!*
    My baby!—the baby I love.

        HARRIET McEWEN KIMBALL in *Wide Awake.*

## FIVE LITTLE CHICKENS.

SAID the first little chicken,
  With a queer little squirm,
"Oh, I wish could find
  A fat little worm!"

Said the next little chicken,
  With an odd little shrug,
"Oh, I wish I could find
  A fat little bug!"

Said the third little chicken,
  With a sharp little squeal,
"Oh, I wish I could find
  Some nice yellow meal!"

Said the fourth little chicken,
  With a small sigh of grief,
"I wish I could find
  A green little leaf!"

Said the fifth little chicken,
  With a faint little moan,
"I wish I could find
  A wee gravel stone!"

"Now, see here," said the mother,
  From the green garden patch,
"If you want any breakfast,
  You must come and scratch."

*American Kindergarten Magazine.*

## MISTRESS KITTY.

MISTRESS KITTY, from the city,
How do your kittens grow?
With eyes so bright,
And fur so white,
And teeth a shining row?

" My kittens white my heart delight,
Their fur is just like snow;
They play and fight
From morn till night;
And *that's* the way they grow."

JENNY WALLIS.

---

## DICK'S SUPPER.

DICK looked out of the window one night,
The moon shone bright,
The round full moon, so silvery white;
"See," cried Dick, "it looks so sweet,
I 'm sure it must be good to eat —
Suppose I take it down to-night,
Just for a treat,
And try one little, little bite!"

Then Dick climbed up on the chimney — so,
The moon hung low,
Bright as silver, and pure as snow;
He snatched it quickly, and cried, "Ho! Ho!

It makes me think of my birthday cake,
All covered with sugar ;
A bite I 'll take,
Just one, and nobody 'll know ! "

But Dickey's mouth was, oh, so wide,
That the moon had nearly slipped inside,
He took such a monstrous bite as you see ;
        But it was n't nice,
        It was colder than ice,
And it made his tooth ache terribly.

" Oh, dear ! oh, dear ! " he began to cry —
" I would n't have the thing, not I ! "
Quickly he hung it again in the sky,
Slid down the chimney, and went to bed.
Then under the blankets he tucked his head ;
" For I know," so he said,
" If anyone thought I had bitten the moon,
I 'd be whipped very soon ! "

But the folks who looked out,
        Of their windows then,
        Both women and men,
        Cried, " Look at the moon !
        It has changed so soon !
When did it get so small, oh, when ? "
And everybody ran out in a fright,
To stare at the bitten moon that night.

Wise men brought their telescopes too,
Old folks their spectacles, — no one knew
What to say, or what to do.

"Ask the almanac-makers," cried one,
"They know everything under the sun!"
But the almanac-makers were quite perplexed,
So they ran to the clerk of the weather next,
Ah, you ought to have seen them run!

Now the clerk of the weather lived all alone,
In a house that was neither wood nor stone;
It had clouds for curtains, and rainbows bright,
Instead of candles, to make it light.
And the pantry shelves were full of jars
Where he kept the snow, the rain, and the stars,
While under the shelves were packed away
Some strong new winds for a stormy day.

The little old man rushed out to see
What on earth could the matter be!
For the people came, with shout and roar,
Thumping and pounding at his door,
Calling loudly, "Come out and tell
What ails our moon?  You know very well."
And sure enough, the moon he saw
Was scooped out like a shell!

The little old man said "Dear, oh, dear!
I can make your weather stormy or clear,
Get up your breezes high or low,
Give you plenty of rain and snow,
Make it hot as you had it last year;
But as for this moon, —
Why, friends, I fear
You have asked me more than I know."

Now all this time poor Dickey was lying
Safe tucked up in his little bed;
And though the toothache kept him crying,
Never a single word he said;
Never told what a monstrous bite
He'd taken out of the moon that night.
So no one ever guessed, or knew,
(Excepting Dickey, and me, and you)
Who gave the folks such a terrible fright.

Mrs. E. T. Corbett in *St. Nicholas.*

---

## FOR THE BABY.

HIDDY–DIDDY! Hiddy-diddy!
　　Ten small chicks, and one old biddy!
"Cluck!" says Biddy, "cluck, cluck, cluck!"
Scratch as I do!—try your luck!"

How the chickens, one and all,
Crowd around her at her call!
One chick, missing, peeps to say,
"Chirp, chirp, chirp!—I've lost my way!"

Shrill and shriller comes the sound!
"Chirp! chirp! chirp! I shall be drowned!"
Biddy clucks, and bustles quick:
"Where, oh, where's my little chick?"

Mister Rooster bustles, too,
Screaming "Cock-a-doodle-doo!
Biddy, I just chanced to look,
And saw your bantling in the brook!"

"Gob!" shrieks Turkey, "gob, gob, gobble!
Mrs. Hen, you're in a hobble!
Why don't some one stir about,
And help your little chicken out?"

"Moo!" roars Sukey, "moo, moo, moo!
What is there that I can do?"
"Uff!" grunts piggy, "uff, uff, uff!
Say you're sorry, that's enough."

"Quack!" says Ducky, "quack, quack, quack!
I have brought your chicken back!"
"Oh!" says Biddy, "cluck, cluck, cluck!
Thank you!—thank you! Mrs. Duck!"

*St. Nicholas.*

## OVER IN THE MEADOW.

OVER in the meadow,
  In the sand, in the sun,
Lived an old mother-toad
  And her little toadie one.
"Wink!" said the mother;
  "I wink," said the one;
So she winked, and she blinked,
  In the sand, in the sun.

Over in the meadow,
  Where the stream runs blue,
Lived an old mother-fish
  And her little fishes two.

"Swim!" said the mother;
  "We swim," said the two;
So they swam, and they leaped,
  Where the stream runs blue.


Over in the meadow,
  In a hole in a tree,
Lived a mother blue-bird
  And her little birdies three.
"Sing!" said the mother;
  "We sing," said the three;
So they sang, and were glad,
  In the hole in the tree.


Over in the meadow,
  In the reeds on the shore,
Lived a mother musk-rat
  And her little ratties four.
"Dive!" said the mother;
  "We dive," said the four;
So they dived, and they burrowed,
  In the reeds on the shore.


Over in the meadow,
  In a snug bee-hive,
Lived a mother honey-bee
  And her little honeys five.
"Buzz!" said the mother;
  "We buzz," said the five;
So they buzzed, and they hummed,
  In the snug bee-hive.

Over in the meadow,
  In a nest built of sticks,
Lived a black mother crow
  And her little crows six.
"Caw!" said the mother;
  "We caw," said the six;
So they cawed, and they called,
  In their nest built of sticks.

Over in the meadow,
  Where the grass is so even,
Lived a gay mother cricket
  And her little crickets seven.
"Chirp!" said the mother;
  "We chirp," said the seven;
So they chirped cheery notes
  In the grass soft and even.

Over in the meadow,
  By the old mossy gate,
Lived a brown mother lizard
  And her little lizards eight.
"Bask!" said the mother;
  "We bask," said the eight;
So they basked in the sun
  On the old mossy gate.

Over in the meadow,
  Where the clear pools shine,
Lived a green mother frog
  And her little froggies nine.

"Croak!" said the mother;
  "We croak," said the nine;
So they croaked, and they plashed,
  Where the clear pools shine.

Over in the meadow,
  In a sly little den,
Lived a gray mother spider
  And her little spiders ten.
"Spin!" said the mother;
  "We spin," said the ten;
So they spun lace webs
  In their sly little den.

Over in the meadow,
  In the soft summer even,
Lived a mother fire-fly
  And her little flies eleven.
"Shine!" said the mother;
  "We shine," said the eleven;
So they shone like stars
  In the soft summer even.

Over in the meadow,
  Where the men dig and delve,
Lived a wise mother ant
  And her little anties twelve.
"Toil!" said the mother;"
  "We toil," said the twelve;
So they toiled, and were wise,
  Where the men dig and delve.

OLIVE A. WADSWORTH.

# THE HANG-BIRD'S NEST.

## A CRADLE SONG.

ROCK-A-BY, birdies, upon the elm tree,
   When the long limbs wave gently and free;
Tough as a bowstring, and drooping and small,
Nothing can break them to give you a fall.
Rock-a-by, birdies, along with the breeze,
All the leaves over you humming like bees.
High away, low away, come again, go!
Go again, come again, rock-a-by-low!

Wonder how papa bird braided that nest,
Binding the twigs about close to his breast;
Wonder how many there are in your bed,
Bonny swung cradle, hung far overhead.
Never mind, birdies, how highly it swings,
Mother bird covers you close with her wings.
High away, low away, come again, go!
Go again, come again, rock-a-by-low!

Rock-a-by, birdies, there 's no one to tire;
Mother rides with you, her wings are like fire:
All the bright feathers are round you so warm.
Rain cannot reach you and wind cannot harm.
Pretty bird babies, let baby go swing
In your high cradle, while mamma shall sing:
High away, low away, come again, go!
Go again, come again, rock-a-by-low!

GEORGE S. BURLEIGH.

# THE CHICKEN'S MISTAKE.

A LITTLE chick one day
  Asked leave to go on the water,
Where she saw a duck, with her brood at play,
  Swimming and splashing about her.

"Indeed," she began to peep and cry,
  When her mother would n't let her,
"If the ducks can swim there, why can't I?
  Are they any bigger or better?"

Then the old hen answered, "Listen to me,
  And hush your foolish talking;
Just look at your feet, and you will see
  They were only made for walking."

But chicky wistfully eyed the brook,
  And did n't half believe her,
For she seemed to say by a knowing look,
  Such stories could n't deceive her.

And, as her mother was scratching the ground,
  She muttered, lower and lower,
"I know I can go there and not be drowned,
  And so I think I'll show her."

Then she made a plunge where the stream was deep,
  And saw too late her blunder;
For she had n't hardly time to peep,
  When her foolish head went under.

And now I hope her fate will show
   The child my story reading,
That those who are older sometimes know,
   What you will do well for heeding;

That each content in his place should dwell,
   And envy not his brother;
And any part that is acted well,
   Is just as good as another.

For we all have our proper sphere below,
   And this is a truth worth knowing:
You will come to grief if you try to go
   Where you were never made for going.

PHEBE CARY.

---

## CAUSE FOR COMPLAINT.

"I DON'T like grandma at all," said Fred,—
   "I don't like grandma at all;"
And he drew his face in a queer grimace,
   The tears were ready to fall,
As he gave his kitten a loving hug,
And disturbed her nap on the soft, warm rug.

"Why, what has your grandma done," I asked,
   "To trouble the little boy?
Oh, what has she done, the cruel one,
   To scatter the smiles of joy?"
Through quivering lips the answer came,
"She — called — my — kitty — a — horrid — name!"

" She did? are you sure?" and I kissed the tears
   Away from the eyelids wet;
" I can scarce believe that grandma could grieve
   The feelings of either pet.
What did she say?"  " Boo-hoo," cried Fred,
" She — called — my — kitten — a — quad — ru — ped!"

JOSEPHINE POLLARD in Harper's Young People.

———◆———

## THE LITTLE PEOPLE.

A DREARY place would be this earth,
   Were there no little people in it;
The song of life would lose its mirth,
   Were there no children to begin it.


No little forms, like buds to grow,
   And make the admiring heart surrender;
No little hands, on breast and brow,
   To keep the thrilling love-cords tender.


The sterner souls would grow more stern,
   Unfeeling nature more inhuman,
And man to stoic coldness turned,
   And woman would be less than woman.


Life's song, indeed, would lose its charm,
   Were there no babies to begin it;
A doleful place this world would be,
   Were there no little people in it.

J. G. WHITTIER.

## THE VILLAINOUS SPIDER.

A SPIDER, grim and old and gray,
  Lived in an apple tree;
He spun his web, and watched for prey—
  "Aha! Oho!" said he.

And when he captured, unaware,
  A moth, or home-bound bee,
He hastened down his fine-spun stair—
  "Aha! Oho!" said he.

Many, many, a gauzy wing,
  In vain tried to get free;
This spider was a wicked thing—
  "Aha! Oho!" said he.

And when his silken web was spun,
  Up in the apple tree;
I'll tell you what he did for fun—
  "Aha! Oho!" said he.

When little Tot was walking out
  One day, with Nancy Lee,
He thought he'd show he was about—
  "Aha! Oho!" said he.

So down he pounced on one fine thread,
  Poor little Tot to see,
And almost touched her curly head—
  "Aha! Oho!" said he.

"Go 'way!" she said, "you ugly thing!
  Go 'way, you frighten me ;
We can't go by, for there you swing" —
  "Aha! Oho!" said he.

So little Totty turned away,
  With lovely Nancy Lee,
And could not go to walk that day —
  "Aha! Oho!" said he.

And when he found this fun was past,
  He scampered up the tree,
And saw a dismal fly caught fast —
  "Aha! Oho!" said he.

*Holly Berries.*

———◆———

## LITTLE WILLIE AND THE APPLE.

LITTLE Willie stood under an apple tree old ;
  The fruit was all shining with crimson and gold,
Hanging temptingly low — how he longed for a bite !
Though he knew if he took one, it would n't be right.

Said he : "I don't see why my father should say,
'Don't touch the old apple tree, Willie, to-day ;'
I should n't have thought, now, they 're hanging so low,
When I asked for just one, he should answer me, 'No.'

"He would never find out if I took but just one ;
And they do look so good, shining out in the sun.
There are hundreds, and hundreds, and he would n't miss
So paltry a little red apple as this."

He stretched forth his hand, but a low, mournful strain,
Came wandering dreamily over his brain;
In his bosom a beautiful harp had long laid,
That the angel of conscience quite frequently played.

And he sung: "Little Willie, beware! oh, beware!
Your father has gone, but your Maker is there;
How sad you would feel if you heard the Lord say,
'This dear little boy stole an apple to-day.'"

Then Willie turned round, and, as still as a mouse,
Crept slowly and carefully into the house.
In his own little chamber he knelt down to pray,
That the Lord would forgive him, and please not to say,
"Little Willie *almost* stole an apple to-day."

## THE LOST KITE.

MY kite! my kite! I've lost my kite!
   Oh, when I saw its airy flight,
How could I know, that letting go
That silly string, would bring so low,
My pretty, buoyant, darling kite,
To pass forever from my sight?
A purple cloud was sailing by,
With silver fringes o'er the sky;
And then I thought it looked so nigh,
I'd let my kite go up, and light
Upon its edge, so soft and bright;
To see how noble, high, and proud she'd look,
When riding on a cloud.

As towards her shining mark she drew,
I clapped my hands, the line slipped through
My silly fingers, and she flew,
Away, away, in airy play,
Right over where the water lay ;
She veered, and fluttered, swung, —
Then gave a plunge — and vanished with the wave.

---

## THE CLEAN FACE.

OH, why must my face be washed so clean,
　　And scrubbed and drenched, for Sunday,
When you very well know, as you've always seen,
　'T will be dirty again on Monday ?

My hair is stiff with the lathery soap,
　That behind my ears is dripping;
And my smarting eyes I'm afraid to ope,
　And my lip the suds is sipping.

They're down my throat, and up my nose,
　And to choke me you seem to be trying;
That I'll shut my mouth you need n't suppose,
　For how can I keep from crying ?

And you rub as hard as ever you can,
　And your hands are hard, to my sorrow ;
No woman shall wash me when I'm a man,
　And I wish I were one to-morrow.

E. LESLIE.

# THE LITTLE BLACK.

LITTLE girls, and little boys,
     If you will not make a noise,
But be quiet as the mice,
I will tell you something nice.

Once there was a little black,
With no clothes upon his back,
By his cruel mother's hand,
Put alive into the sand.

Wandering from a shady wood,
Came a missionary good,
Who, as he was passing by,
Heard a little feeble cry.

Then he stooped, and scratched the sand.
First he saw a little hand,
Then a little mouth and nose,
And such cunning little toes.

Then he scratched the sand about;
And he pulled the baby out;
And he took it to his wife,
Who preserved its little life.

'Twas a little girl I'm told,
And it was as good as gold;
And he kept it till it grew
Quite as big as some of you.

Then to England it was sent,
With the kind and good intent,
That, when taught, it might go back
To instruct the little black.

If the missionary good
Had not wandered from the wood,
Had not listened when it cried,
Little baby would have died.

And, if such had been the case,
Then the news of gospel grace
Those poor children might not reach,
Whom this little girl will teach.

Little girls, and little boys,
God the meanest things employs
To perform the greatest deeds,
And accomplish what he needs.

Then let every child to-day,
Turning to his neighbor say,
"Who can tell but you and I
Can do something, if we try?"

## WHAT THE CHOIR SANG ABOUT THE NEW BONNET.

A FOOLISH little maiden bought a foolish little bonnet,
  With a ribbon, and a feather, and a bit of lace upon it;
And, that the other maidens of the little town might
    know it,
She thought she'd go to meeting the next Sunday, just
    to show it.

But though the little bonnet was scarce larger than a dime,
The getting of it settled, proved to be a work of time;
So when 'twas fairly tied, all the bells had stopped their
    ringing,
And when she came to meeting, sure enough, the folks
    were singing.

So this foolish little maiden stood and waited at the door,
And she shook her ruffles out behind, and smoothed them
    down before.
"Hallelujah! hallelujah!" sang the choir above her head,
"Hardly knew you! hardly knew you!" were the words
    she thought they said.

This made the little maiden feel so very, very cross,
That she gave her little mouth a twist, her little head a
    toss;
For she thought the very hymn they sang, was all about
    her bonnet,
With the ribbon, and the feather, and the bit of lace
    upon it.

And she would not wait to listen to the sermon, or the
    prayer,
But pattered down the silent street, and hurried up the
    stair,
Till she reached her little bureau, and, in a band-box on it,
Had hidden, safe from critic's eye, her foolish little bonnet.

Which proves, my little maidens, that each of you will find
In every Sabbath service but an echo of your mind;
And the silly little head, that's filled with silly little airs,
Will never get a blessing, from sermon or from prayers.

Miss Hammond.

---

## MY SPEECH.

PRAY, how shall I, a little lad, in speaking make a
    figure?
You 're only joking, I 'm afraid, do wait till I am bigger.
But since you wish to hear my part, and urge me to begin
    it,
I 'll strive for praise with all my heart, though small the
    hope to win it.
I 'll tell a tale, how farmer John a little roan colt bred, sir.
Which every night and every morn, he watered, and he
    fed, sir;
Said neighbor Joe, to farmer John, "Are n't you a silly
    dolt, sir;
To spend such time and care, upon a useless little colt,
    sir?"
Said farmer John, to neighbor Joe, "I bring my little roan
    up,

Not for the good he can do now, but will do when he's
    grown up."
The moral you can well espy, to keep the tale from
    spoiling ;
The little colt you think is I, I know it by your smiling.
And now, my friends, please to excuse my lisping, and my
    stammers ;
I for this once have done my best, so now I'll make my
    manners.

---

## HOPPIE-OPPIE.

HOPPIE-OPPIE was my pet,
    In my mind I see him yet ;
His eyes so big ! his mouth so wide !
His spots ! in which he took such pride !

In a glass jar he grew apace,
And o'er the mouth we drew some lace ;
Then flies I caught, and pushed them through
A little hole — alive — 't is *true.*

With hop and jump, he'd snap them up,
With him 'twas always time to sup ;
With pleasure then he'd gaily wink,
'T was very saucy, so I think.

He never failed his bath to take,
And boldly then his plunge did make ;
His coat now shone, his color rose
He polished up his little toes.

Upon my hand, in room or hall,
I'd hold him up quite near the wall,
Wherever I could see a fly;
He gave them not a chance to sigh.

About my room he'd daily hop,
And in a corner he would stop;
He jumped through chairs without a fear;
When puzzled, he would scratch his ear.

If flies were dead, he scorned to eat,
And trod them down beneath his feet.
One day I played on him a trick,
And kept one stirring, with a stick.

(Alas, I fear it was a sin.)
He eyed it close, then popped it in;
I fancied, as he tossed it down,
He gave me just one little frown.

The flies grew scarce.  So fast he grew,
I found I must try something new.
I dug fat worms, — his eyes grew bright,
And quick they vanished from my sight.

At worsted monkeys he would jump,
And on the floor fall with a thump;
This twice he tried, the third time he
Would scratch his ear, and turn to me.

To Prospect Park I carried him;
On mossy bank, 'neath spreading limb,
I left him, to his great surprise;
No doubt he still is catching flies.

Then don't despise the little toad,
That oft near man makes his abode;
He does the work for which he's made,
Better than you do, I'm afraid.

JENNY WALLIS.

## FOR THE LITTLE ONES.

WHAT says the clock when it strikes one?
    "Watch," says the clock, "Oh, watch little one!"
What says the clock when it strikes two?
"Love God, little darling, for God loves you."
And tell me, tell me softly, what it whispers at three?
It is, "Suffer little children to come unto me."
Then come, gentle darlings, come, and wonder no more,
'Tis the voice of the shepherd that calls thee at four;
And oh, let your young hearts with gladness revive,
When it echoes, so sweetly, "God bless thee!" at five.
And remember at six, at the waning of day,
That your life is a vapor, that passeth away.
What says the clock when it strikes seven?
"Of such is the kingdom, the kingdom of heaven."
What says the clock when it strikes eight?
"Strive, strive to enter at the beautiful gate."
And louder, still louder, it calls thee at nine;
And its voice is, "My child, give me that heart of thine."
Then loud be your voices responsive at ten,
"Hosanna in the highest, Hosanna, Amen!"
Then loud let the chorus ring on till eleven,
Praise, praise to the Father, the Father in Heaven!
While the deep stroke of midnight the watchword shall bring,
Lo, these are my jewels, these, these, saith the King.

## THE LITTLE DOG UNDER THE WAGON.

"COME, wife," says good old Farmer Gray,
  "Put on your things, 't is market day;
Let's be off to the nearest town,—
There and back ere the sun goes down.
*Spot?* No, we'll leave old Spot behind."
But Spot he barked, and Spot he whined,
And soon made up his doggish mind
    To steal away under the wagon.

Away they went, a good round pace,
And joy came into the farmer's face.
"Poor Spot," said he, *did* want to come;
But I'm very glad he's left at home.
He'll guard the barn, and guard the cot,
And keep the cattle out of the lot."
"I'm not so sure of that," growled Spot,—
    The little dog under the wagon.

The farmer all his produce sold,
And got his pay in yellow gold;
Then started home, just after dark,—
Home through the lonely forest.  Hark!
A robber sprang from behind a tree;
"Your money or else your life!" said he.
The moon was out, yet he didn't see
    The little dog under the wagon.

Old Spot he barked, and Spot he whined,
And Spot he grabbed the thief behind,

And dragged him down in mud and dirt.
He tore his coat, and tore his shirt,
And held him with a whisk and bound ;
And he could n't rise from the miry ground ;
While his legs and arms the farmer bound.
    And tumbled him into the wagon.

Old Spot he saved the farmer's life,
The farmer's money, the farmer's wife ;
And now a hero, grand and gay,
A silver collar he wears to-day ;
And everywhere his master goes,
Among his friends, among his foes,
He follows upon his horny toes,—
    The little dog under the wagon.

Mrs. M. A. Kidder.

## SPINNING.

A SPIDER was swinging herself in glee
    From a moss-covered swaying bough ;
A breeze came rollicking up from the sea,
    And fanned her beautiful brow.
She hung, it is true, with her pretty head down,
    But her brain was cool as you please ;
The fashion quite suited the cut of her gown,
    And she could look up in the trees.

She saw where a humming-bird lighted down ;
    At his throat a bright ruby gleamed ;
On his head was a gold and emerald crown,
    And he sat on a bough and dreamed.

The spider ran up on her silver thread,
    And looked in the little king's face ;
" If I may but sit at your feet," she said,
    " I 'll spin you some beautiful lace."

The humming-bird looked in her shining eyes,
    And then at her nimble feet,
And said to himself, I have found a prize,
    She is useful as well as neat.
" You may sit by my side, if it please you well,"
    Said he, "the summer-time through ;
And since you spin on a noiseless wheel,
    I 'll do the humming for you."

                MARIAN DOUGLASS in *Our Young Folks.*

---

## A BOY'S AND GIRL'S WAY.

CHILDREN, stop your play,
        And tell me which way
I shall take to reach the city on the hill ?

            First the girl,
            With a smile :
            " This way,
Through the woods, across the stile,
    By a brook where wild flowers grow,
    Where the birds sing sweet and low ;
        Then you forget it is so far,
        And how tired you are ;
For the calm rests you, makes you still,
If you take this way to the city on the hill."

Then the boy,
  With a frown:
  "This way,
By the mill, and through the town, —
  You will see the soldiers there,
  Hear the drums, and pass the fair;
    Then you forget the way is long,
    While you walk in the throng;
For the noise wakes you, makes you thrill,
When you go this way to the city on the hill."

———◆———

## A DINNER AND A KISS.

"I HAVE brought your dinner, father,"
  The blacksmith's daughter said,
As she took from her arms a kettle,
  And lifted its shining lid.
"There's not any pie or pudding,
  So I will give you this ——;"
And upon his toil-worn forehead
  She left a childish kiss.

The blacksmith tore off his apron,
  And dined in happy mood,
Wondering much at the savor
  Hid in his humble food,
While all about him were visions
  Full of prophetic bliss;
But he never thought of the magic
  In his little daughter's kiss.

While she with her kettle swinging,
  Merrily trudged away,
Stopping at sight of a squirrel,
  Catching some wild bird's lay;
And I thought how many a shadow
  Of life and fate we would miss,
If always our frugal dinners
  Were seasoned with a kiss.

*Pittsburg Commercial.*

## THE RAINY DAY.

GENTLY now the rain is falling;
  Hark! I hear the children calling,
"Auntie, dear, please tell a story, —
Not about 'Old Mother Morey;'

"But about some fairy queen,
Who in brilliant robes was seen,
With a group of merry sprites,
'Neath the harvest moon o' nights.

"She must have a little car,
On her head must shine a star,
She must give us wishes three,
While they dance around the tree."

"I," said Maud, "will choose a bird,
If she will listen to my word;
A gilded cage and music sweet,
My eyes and ears shall early greet."

"I will choose a talking doll,
With velvet robes and parasol;
A little carriage, too, beside,
Wherein she oft shall take a ride," —

Thus said little Isabel,
With cheek like faintly tinted shell;
While Jack spoke out, "I'll choose a top,
A whip, and horse that'll never stop,

"But bear me swiftly thro' the town,
And o'er the fields, and then go down
Where I shall find that pot o' gold,
At rainbow's end, as often told."

Then Helen said, "I choose the story
That's not about 'Old Mother Morey;'"
But, with their chat, the hours had fled,
And soon for them 't was time for bed.

JENNY WALLIS.

—◆—

## PRIDE GOES BEFORE A FALL.

AS forth I walked, one wintry day,
    To view the merry sport
Of laughing children at their play,
    Beyond our little court,

I saw a tiny little maid,
    In furs and velvet drest,
Whose every motion plainly said,
    "I'm in my very best."

'T is said, " Pride goes before a fall."
　　I think it must be so ;
For soon this maiden, far from tall,
　　Slipped down upon the snow.

I then sprang quickly to her aid,
　　And placed her on her feet.
"Poor little girl!" I gently said,
　　"I hope you are not hurt."

"I 'm hurt," she said, "for hard I fell,
　　But poor I 'm not," she cried.
"I 've money more than I can tell,
　　And lovely clothes beside."

I could but smile at her mistake,
　　And soon she passed from view ;
While I resolved my pen to take,
　　And share my mirth with you.

JENNY WALLIS.

---

## THE EARLY WORM.

"COME, little pet," the old bird said,
　　In most endearing term,
"You must be early out of bed
　　If you would catch the worm."

The smallest of the feathery herd, —
　　A puny little thing, —
Out sprang the tender baby-bird,
　　To grub for worms, and sing.

And lo! she found an early worm —
  It was a monster, too —
She chirped, "Oh, you may writhe and squirm,
  But I will gobble you!"


That birdling's chirp, the rest affirm,
  Was never after heard ;
And it 's surmised it was the worm
  That caught the early bird.


## KITTY.

ALAS! little Kitty — do give her your pity! —
  Had lived seven years, and was never called pretty!
Her hair was bright red, and her eyes were dull blue,
    And her cheeks were so freckled,
    They looked like the speckled
Wild lilies, that down in the meadow-land grew.
If her eyes had been black, if she'd only had curls,
She had been, so she thought, the most happy of girls.


Her cousins around her, they pouted and fretted,
But they were all pretty, and they were all petted ;
While poor little Kitty, though striving her best
    To do her child's duty,
    Not sharing their beauty,
Was always neglected, and never caressed.
All in vain, so she thought, was she loving and true,
While her hair was bright red, and her eyes were dull blue,

But one day, alone, 'mid the clover blooms sitting,
She heard a strange sound, as of wings round her flitting;
A light not of sunbeams, a fragrance more sweet
      Than the winds blowing over
      The red-blossomed clover,
Made her thrill with delight, from her head to her feet;
And a voice low and rare, whispered low in the air,
"See that beautiful, beautiful child sitting there!"

Thrice blessed little Kitty! She almost looked pretty!
Beloved by the angels, she needed no pity!
O juvenile charmers, with shoulders of snow,
      Ruby lips, sunny tresses,
      Forms made for caresses,
There's one thing, my beauties, 't is well you should know:
Though the world is in love with bright eyes and soft hair,
It is only *good* children the angels call fair.

MARIAN DOUGLASS in *Our Young Folks.*

---

## THE FAIRY'S RESCUE.

GOOD luck for me!
   There's a humble-bee
Rolling in the clover;
Hay-seed, fly over
And catch him for me.

I must take a ride to day
O'er the waves of blooming hay.
Up the hill-side, in the glen,
Live two little, elvish men.

Their beards are white, their beards are long,
Their hands are big, their hands are strong;
They 've got my baby in their den,
The hateful, hateful elvish men!
They rode on a long-tailed dragon-fly,
And they soared low, and they soared high;
    They snatched her up
    From a buttercup,
    And carried her off
    With squeal and scoff.


They 'll make her toil, they make her slave,
Their hoards of blossom-dust to save;
They 'll harness her with beetles, too,
To drag their acorn-cups of dew.
    Get up, humble-bee!
Or I'll tickle thy furry thigh
With this beard of golden rye —
    Get up, humble-bee!


    Buzz! buzz! hum! hum!
    Here I come!
I've got her! The hateful, elvish men
Shall never, never find her again.


I stormed their den with my humble-bee;
With his big, sharp lance he fought for me.
We tore their walls of rotting bark,
We chased them into their dungeon dark;
With strong pine needles we barred them in,
There they shall stay till they rue their sin.

I found my darling with smutty wings,
And spotted with cruel nettle-stings;
But I've swung her through the waterfall's mist,
And a cleaner darling never was kissed.
I'll put her to bed in the grass down deep,
And set the crickets to sing her to sleep.

ANNETTE BISHOP in Riverside Magazine.

---

## THE DONATION PARTY.

THEY carried pie to the parson's house,
    And scattered the floor with crumbs,
And marked the leaves of his choicest books
    With the prints of their greasy thumbs.

They piled his dishes high and thick
    With a lot of unhealthy cake,
While they gobbled the buttered toast and rolls,
    Which the parson's wife did make.

They hung around Clytie's classic neck
    Their apple-parings for sport,
And every one laughed when a clumsy lout
    Spilled his tea in the pianoforte.

Next day the parson went down on his knees,
    With his wife — but not to pray;
Oh, no, 't was to scrape the grease and dirt
    From the carpet and stairs away.

## BEFORE AND AFTER SCHOOL.

### BEFORE SCHOOL.

"QUARTER to nine! Boys and girls, do you hear?"
    "One more buckwheat, then; be quick, mother dear!"
"Where is my luncheon-box?" "Under the shelf,
Just in the place where you left it yourself."
"I can't say my table!" "Oh, find me my cap!"
"One kiss for mamma, and sweet sis in her lap."
"Be good, dear!" "I'll try." "9 times 9's 81."
"Take your mittens!" "All right! Hurry up, Bill, let's
        run!"
With a slam of the door they are off, girls and boys,
And the mother draws breath in the lull of their noise.

### AFTER SCHOOL.

"Don't wake up the baby! Come gently, my dear!"
"O mother, I've torn my new dress; just look here!
I'm sorry! I only was climbing a wall."
"Oh, mother, my map was the nicest of all;
And Nelly, in spelling, went up to the head!"
"Oh, say, can I go out on the hill with my sled?"
"I've got such a toothache!" "The teacher's unfair!"
"Is dinner most ready? I'm just like a bear!"
Be patient, worn mother, they're growing up fast;
These nursery whirlwinds, not long do they last.
A still, lonely house would be far worse than noise;
Rejoice and be glad in your brave girls and boys.

*R. I. Schoolmaster.*

## WHY SOME BIRDS HOP AND OTHERS WALK.

A LITTLE bird sat on a twig of a tree,
  A swinging and singing as glad as could be,
And shaking his tail, and smoothing his dress,
And having such fun as you never could guess.

And when he had finished his gay little song,
He flew down in the street, and went hopping along,
This way and that way, with both little feet,
While his sharp little eyes looked for something to eat

A little boy said to him : "Little bird, stop,
And tell me the reason you go with a hop.
Why don't you walk, as boys do, and men,
One foot at a time, like a dove or a hen ? "

Then the little bird went with a hop, hop, hop ;
And he laughed and he laughed as he never would stop ;
And he said : "Little boy, there are some birds that talk,
And some birds that hop, and some birds that walk.

"Use your eyes, little boy : watch closely and see
What little birds hop, both feet, just like me,
And what little birds walk like the duck and the hen ;
And when you know that, you 'll know more than some men.

"Every bird that can scratch in the dirt can walk ;
Every bird that can wade in the water can walk ;
Every bird that has claws to catch prey with can walk ;
One foot at a time, — that is why they can walk.

"But most little birds who can sing you a song,
Are so small, that their legs are not very strong
To scratch with, or wade with, or catch things, — that's
     why
They hop with both feet.* Little boy, good-by."

J. L. BATES in Wide Awake.

—◆—

## A RELIC OF "THE FOURTH."

I HEARD a mother's 'plaining voice,
  "Where is my darling son?
My Charlie had two pearly ears,
  But you have only one.

"My Charlie had upon each hand,
  A thumb, and fingers four;
But you have only four in all,
  And they are blackened o'er.

"My Charlie had a pair of eyes,
  But one have you, strange lad;
And Charlie had a pretty nose,
  I'm sure you never had.

"My boy had brows above his eyes,
  And hair upon his head;
Your face is black as any hat,
  His face was white and red.

* The exceptions to this rule are rare. The rule is generally correct, and so simple
as easily to be remembered.

"My Charley's clothes were new and clean,
    All rags and dirt are yours;
From head to foot you seem to be
    A regiment of sores."

Then shrilly cried that wrecked boy,
    "Don't know me, ma? I say,
I've had the jolliest, biggest time
    Of all my life to-day."

She stoops her down in agony,
    Though sorely she's bereft,
She has a mother's yearning still,
    And clings to what is left.

EDWARD E. EDWARDS in Boston Transcript.

---

## MY WRENS.

HIGH up in my arbor,
    In the month of June,
Jacky Wren is fluttering,
    Singing his sweet tune.

Why is he so happy?
    Why this merry song?
Near him listens Jenny,
    In her nest so strong.

Now she joins her Jacky,
    For a little while;
Fills her bill with tid-bits,
    Over by the stile.

Then to her three birdies
　　Swift returns again ;
The "early worm" she's bringing
　　Soon forgets his pain.

Happy little birdlings,
　　In their tiny nest !
Sure their mother 'll give them
　　Food that suits them best.

　　　　　　　　　JENNY WALLIS.

---

## THE MOTHERLESS TURKEYS.

THE white turkey was dead !　The white turkey was
　　　　dead !
　　How the news through the barnyard went flying !
Of a mother bereft, four small turkeys were left,
　　And their case for assistance was crying.

E'en the peacock respectfully folded his tail,
　　As a beautiful symbol of sorrow ;
And his plainer wife said, "Now the old bird is dead,
　　Who will tend her poor chicks on the morrow ?

"And when evening around them comes dreary and chill,
　　Who above them will watchfully hover ? "
"Two each night I will tuck 'neath my wing," said the
　　　　duck,
　　"Though I 've eight of my own I must cover."

"I have too much to do.  For the bugs and the worms
    In the garden 'tis tiresome pickin';
I have nothing to spare — for my own I must care,"
    Said the hen with only one chicken.

"How I wish," said the goose, "I could be of some use,
    For my heart is with love overbrimming;
The next morning that's fine they shall go with mine,
    Little yellow-back goslings out swimming."

"I will do all I can," the old Dorking put in,
    "And for help they may call upon me, too;
Though I've ten of my own that are only half-grown,
    And a great deal of trouble to see to;

"But those poor little things, they are all head and wings,
    And their bones through their feathers are stickin'."
"Very hard, it may be; but, oh, don't come to me!"
    Said the hen with only one chicken.

"Half my care, I suppose, there is nobody knows;
    I'm the most overburdened of mothers.
They must learn, little elves, how to scratch for themselves,
    And not seek to depend upon others."

She went by with a cluck; and the goose to the duck
    Exclaimed in surprise, "Well, I never!"
Said the duck, "I declare, those who have the least care,
    You will find, are complaining forever.

"And when all things appear to look threatening and drear,
    And when troubles your pathway are thick in,
For aid in your woes, oh, beware how you go
    To a hen with only one chicken!"

                                        MARIAN DOUGLASS.

## THE LITTLE CONQUEROR.

"'TWAS midnight; not a sound was heard
    Within the —" "Papa, won't 'ou 'ook
An' see my pooty 'ittle house?
    I wis' 'ou would n't wead 'ou book —"

"Within the palace, where the king
    Upon his couch in anguish lay —"
"Papa, Pa-*pa!* I wis' 'ou'd tum
    An' have a 'ittle tonty play —"

"No gentle hand was there to bring
    The cooling draught, or bathe his brow;
His courtiers and his pages gone —"
    "Tum, papa, tum; I want 'ou *now* —"

Down goes the book with needless force;
    And, with expression far from mild,
With sullen air and clouded brow,
    I seat myself beside the child.

Her little trusting eyes of blue
    With mute surprise gaze in my face,
As if, in its expression stern,
    Reproof and censure she could trace.

Anon her little bosom heaves,
    Her rosy lips begin to curl;
And, with a quivering chin, she sobs,
    "Papa don't 'uv his 'ittle dirl."

King, palace, book — all are forgot ;
　My arms are round my darling thrown ;
The thundercloud has burst, and, lo !
　Tears fall, and mingle with her own.

CHARLES FOLLEN ADAMS, in Gems for the Fireside.

———◆———

## A SUM IN ARITHMETIC.

THERE came into our school one day,
　A white-haired. man, with pleasant smile ;
He greeted us, and, sitting down,
Said he would like to rest awhile.


'T was time to have arithmetic.
The teacher said, "Now all give heed !
Put up your books, and take your slates,
And do the sum which I will read."


Our books went in, our slates came out,
And the teacher read the sum.
We tried and tried, and tried again,
And could n't make the answer come.


And then the old man said to us,
With kindness twinkling in his eyes,
"Who gets the answer first, shall have
A silver shilling for a prize."

Then Tommy Dole resolved to cheat;
And slyly taking out his book,
When he supposed he was not seen,
A hasty glance inside he took.

At once the answer Tommy finds,
And, "Now I've got it, sir," he cries.
The teacher thinks Tom worked the sum,
And tells him he has won the prize.

But that old man had seen it all,
Those twinkling eyes had watched the trick.
"Well done, my boy! you seem
To understand arithmetic.

"But now, before I give the prize,
I'll let you try a harder one.
Another shilling you shall have,
If you can tell how that is done."

And then, with kindest voice and look,
He gently said to Tommy Dole,
"What shall it profit you, my lad,
To gain the world, and lose your soul?"

Then Tommy Dole hung down his head,
And tears began to fill his eyes;
And all the scholars wondered why
He would not take the silver prize.

## THE HERO.

MY father was a farmer good,
　With corn and beef in plenty;
I mowed and hoed, and held the plough,
　And longed for one-and-twenty;
For I had quite a martial turn,
　And scorned the lowing cattle;
I burned to wear a uniform,
　Hear drums, and see a battle.

My birthday came; my father urged,
　But stoutly I resisted;
My sister wept, my mother prayed;
　But off I went and 'listed.
They marched me on, through wet and dry,
　To tunes more loud than charming;
But lugging knapsack, box, and gun,
　Was harder work than farming.

We met the foe, — the cannon roared,
　The crimson tide was flowing,
The frightful death-groans filled my ears,
　I wished that I were mowing.
I lost my leg — the foe came on,
　They had me in their clutches;
I starved in prison till the peace,
　Then hobbled home on crutches.

## SUPPOSE!

SUPPOSE, my little lady,
　　Your doll should break his head,
Could you make it whole by crying
　　Till your nose and eyes are red?
And would n't it be pleasanter
　　To treat it as a joke,
And say you're glad "t' was Dolly's,
　　And not your head that broke?"

Suppose you're dressed for walking,
　　And the rain comes pouring down,
Will it clear off any sooner
　　Because you scold and frown?
And would n't it be nicer
　　For you to smile than pout,
And so make sunshine in the house,
　　When there is none without?

Suppose your task, my little man,
　　Is very hard to get,
Will it make it any easier
　　For you to sit and fret?
And would n't it be wiser,
　　Than waiting like a dunce,
To go to work in earnest,
　　And learn the thing at once?

Suppose that some boys have a horse,
    And some a coach and pair,
Will it tire you less, while walking,
    To say, " It is n't fair ? "
And would n't it be nobler
    To keep your temper sweet,
And in your heart be thankful
    You can walk upon your feet.

And suppose the world don't please you,
    Nor the way some people do,
Do you think the whole creation
    Will be altered just for you?
And is n't it, my boy or girl,
    The wisest, bravest plan,
Whatever comes or does n't come,
    To do the best you can?

                                    ALICE CARY.

—◆—

## WHISTLE AND HOE.

THERE'S a boy just over the garden fence,
    Who is whistling all through the livelong day;
And his work is not just a mere pretence,
    For you see the weeds he has cut away.
            Whistle and hoe,
            Sing as you go,
            Shorten the row
            By the songs you know.

Not a word of bemoaning his task I hear;
  He has scarcely time for a growl, I know;
For his whistle sounds so merry and clear,
  He must find some pleasure in every row.
       Whistle and hoe,
       Sing as you go,
       Shorten the row
       By the songs you know.

But then, while you whistle, be sure that you hoe,
  For if you are idle the briars will spread;
And whistle alone to the end of the row
  May do for the weeds, but is bad for the bread.
       Whistle and hoe,
       Sing as you go,
       Shorten the row
       By the songs you know.

*Rural New Yorker.*

---

## THE FOUR PRESENTS.

I HAD four brothers over the sea,
  And they each sent a present unto me.

The first sent a goose without a bone;
The second a cherry without a stone;

The third sent a blanket without a thread;
The fourth sent a book that no man could read.

When the cherry's in the blossom, there is no stone;
When the goose is in the egg-shell, there is no bone;

When the wool's on the sheep's back, there's no thread;
When the book's in the press, no man it can read.

*The Baby's Bouquet.*

---

## A COMPLAINT.

MY name is Grasshopper.   High as I can
    Here I hop, there I hop, — little old man!
Look at my countenance, aged and thin;
Look at my crooked legs, all doubled in;
Is not my face long and sober and wan?
Do I not look like a little old man?
Yet all the summer I play in the grass,
Jump up and stick to whoever may pass,
Where I then hide myself they cannot guess, —
Never know where I am till they undress.
Finger and thumb then they snap me away,
Though they might know how much rather I'd stay.
Nobody cares what becomes of poor me;
Flung out of window I'm certain to be,
E'en though the hen might be there with her brood!
A Grasshopper's feelings, — they're not understood!

MRS. ANNA M. WELLS, in *Our Young Folks.*

## THE CONSCIENTIOUS HEN.

"DEAR! dear! who broke my favorite egg?"
Cried Biddy Bantam to her daughter.
"Some lazy cur, too proud to beg,
Has mashed it; and he had n't oughter."

The child gave one pathetie craw,
Her rueful tears began to thicken,
She sobbed aloud, "I broke it, ma;
This little person is my chicken.

"Some albumen and lime I 'll buy,
And make another one to match it;
O ma! I cannot tell a lie, —
I did it with my little hatch it."

———◆———

## THE SECRET OF HAPPINESS.

IT is not much the world can give,
With all its subtle art,
And gold and gems are not the things
To satisfy the heart;
But oh, if those who cluster round
The altar and the hearth,
Have gentle words and loving smiles,
How beautiful is earth!

# THE ROBIN.

MY old Welsh neighbor over the way,
　　Crept slowly out in the sun of spring,
Pushed from her ears the locks of gray,
　　And listened to hear the robins sing.

Her grandson, playing at marbles, stopped,
　　And, cruel in sport, as boys will be,
Tossed a stone at the bird, who hopped
　　From bough to bough in the apple tree.

" Nay!" said the grandmother; "have you not heard,
　　My poor, bad boy! of the fiery pit,
And how, drop by drop, this merciful bird
　　Carries the water that quenches it?

" He brings cool dew in his little bill,
　　And lets it fall on the souls of sin:
You can see the mark on his red breast still,
　　Of fires that scorch as he drops it in.

" My poor Bron rhuddyn! my breast-burned bird,
　　Singing so sweetly from limb to limb,
Very dear to the heart of our Lord
　　Is he who pities the lost like him!"

" Amen!" I said to the beautiful myth;
　　" Sing, bird of God, in my heart as well;
Each good thought is a drop wherewith
　　To cool and lessen the fires of hell.

" Prayers of love, like raindrops fall,
　Tears of pity are cooling dew,
And dear to the heart of our Lord are all
　Who suffer like him in the good they do!"

JOHN G. WHITTIER.

---

## GOD WANTS THE BOYS AND GIRLS.

GOD wants the boys, the merry, merry boys,
　　The noisy boys, the funny boys,
　　　　The thoughtless boys.
God wants the boys, with all their joys,
　That he as gold may make them pure,
　And teach them trials to endure.
　　　　His heroes brave
　　　　　He 'll have them be,
　　　　Fighting for truth
　　　　　And purity.
God wants the boys.

God wants the happy-hearted girls,
The loving girls, the best of girls,
　　　　The worst of girls.
God wants to make the girls his pearls,
　And so reflect his holy face,
　And bring to mind his wondrous grace ;
　　　　That beautiful
　　　　　The world may be,
　　　　And filled with love
　　　　　And purity.
God wants the girls.

## MAGIC CURTAINS.

I KNOW of some curtains all lined with pink silk,
    And bordered with fringes of gold,
That, fashioned of satin the hue of rich milk,
    Are made to fold and unfold.
When darkness comes on, and the world sinks to sleep,
    These beautiful curtains slip down,
And all through the night hours caressingly sweep
    The cheeks of the sleepers in town ;
And when the day dawns, and the people wake up,
    These curtains they fold up so tight,
Their creamy-white fulness so closely take up,
    That only the fringe is in sight.
Do you know what these wonderful curtains are yet ?
    Or will you be filled with surprise,
When I tell you that two are most cunningly set
    Right over your wondering eyes ?

---

## SANTA CLAUS AND THE MOUSE.

ONE Christmas Eve, when Santa Claus
    Came to a certain house,
To fill the children's stockings there,
    He found a little mouse.

"A merry Christmas ! little friend,"
    Said Santa, good and kind,
"The same to you, sir !" said the mouse ;
    "I thought you would n't mind

"If I should stay awake to-night,
  And watch you for awhile."
"You're very welcome, little mouse,"
  Said Santa with a smile.

And then he filled the stockings up,
  Before the mouse could wink, —
From toe to top, from top to toe,
  There wasn't left a chink.

"Now they won't hold another thing,"
  Said Santa Claus with pride.
A twinkle came in mouse's eyes,
  But humbly he replied:

"It's not polite to contradict, —
  Your pardon I implore;
But, in the fullest stocking there,
  I could put one thing more."

"Oh, ho!" laughed Santa, "silly mouse!
  Don't I know how to pack?
By filling stockings all these years,
  I should have learned the knack."

And then he took the stocking down
  From where it hung so high,
And said, "Now put in one thing more,
  I give you leave to try."

The mousie chuckled to himself,
  And then he softly stole,
Right to the stocking's crowded toe,
  And gnawed a little hole.

"Now, if you please, good Santa Claus,
  I've put in one thing more,
For you will own, that little hole
  Was not in there before."

How Santa Claus did laugh and laugh!
  And then he gayly spoke,
"Well, you shall have a Christmas cheese
  For that nice little joke!"

Emilie Poulsson, in St. Nicholas.

---

## THE FOOLISH PANSY.

A DAINTY little pansy
    Stood on one toe,
Stretched up her pretty head,
    And wanted to know

Why she was tethered fast,
    Just to one spot,
While zephyrs could wander
    Where she could not.

"O gentle Queen of Fairies,"
    I heard her softly say,
"Please cut the ties that bind me,
    And bid me fly away.

"I know I'm far too pretty
    So hidden here to lie;
To look abroad and see the world,
    I'm sure I'd like to try."

"O foolish little pansy,
  Your choice you're sure to rue;
To soar aloft, on restless wing,
  Is not for such as you."

But the pretty pansy pouted,
  And not a smile was seen,
While sadly leaned above her,
  The gentle Fairy Queen.

So, weary of her sulking,
  At length she waved her wand,
And pansy flew away, away,
  She thought to Fairy-land.

The zephyrs changed to breezes,
  Then fast and faster blew,
And soon beside the river
  The pretty pansy threw.

Then leaning o'er the water,
  She started back in fright;
For, in that faithful mirror,
  She saw a fearful sight.

Her truant ways and temper,
  Had seamed her forehead o'er
With wrinkles and with bruises, —
  Her beauty was no more.

Too late she saw her error,
  Too late she sighed full sore;
She fainted there, and perished
  Upon that pebbly shore.

Thus ends my little story;
   For, down beneath the wave,
This foolish little pansy
   Soon found a lonely grave.

Shall I not take this lesson,
   And feel content to rest
Where God in love has placed me,
   Assured his choice is best?

JENNY WALLIS.

—◆—

## SHUT THE DOOR SOFTLY.

SHUT the door softly, mother's asleep,
   Her fever is broken, her slumber is deep;
Look in her pale face, and see there no pain, —
Darling, be thankful, we've mother again.

Shut the door softly, and come to her side;
What should we do if our mother had died? —
She who has loved us our weary lives through;
Shut the door softly, and do as I do.

Shut the door softly, and kneel with me here,
To Him who has spared us our own mother dear;
Who has given her back to our arms once again,
Borne her through danger, and softened her pain.

Shut the door softly, and look in her face,
And see how it gathered in health and in grace.
Is she not handsome, this mother of ours,
Waking to life like the budding of flowers?

Let us lose all in this fast flying life,
Sister and brother, and husband and wife,
Mother's love only all time has defied;
Shut the door softly, and come to her side.

Shut the door softly, mother's awake,
Back from the shores of the fathomless lake;
Weary with travel, but laden with charms,
Longing to clasp us within her dear arms.

Mother, dear mother! we loved you before,
Now we shall love you a thousand times more;
Welcome, dear heart, from the shadowy land;
Shut the door softly, and kiss her dear hand.

—◆—

## BABY IN THE LOOKING-GLASS.

MY baby boy sat on the floor,
   His big blue eyes were full of wonder;
For he had never thought before,
That baby by the mirror door,
   What kept the two, so near, asunder.

He leaned toward that golden head,
   The mirror border framed within,
Until twin cheeks, like roses red,
Lay side by side, then softly said,
   "I can't get out; can't you come in?"

## HAPPY BIRTHDAY: A TWO-FOLD SONG.

HERE'S twice the greetings two have known,
  With twice the ardor lent to one,
In double measure, doubly done,
    We wish you Happy Birthday!

Ring out your voices twice as clear
As two could make them, twice a year,
Bring twice the love, and twice the cheer,
    To this twice Happy Birthday!

What double tasks to me belong,
With two to swell the twice-told wrong!
How shall I twist my two-fold song,
    To suit this Happy Birthday?

May twice the joys of man below,
Be yours to share, and yours to know;
With two-fold radiance may they glow
    Through many a Happy Birthday!

.May two fast friends, where'er they meet,
This day with two-fold gladness greet,
And two dear lives be made twice sweet,
    Each doubly Happy Birthday!

Though twice as shrill the wild winds blow,
And doubly deep the cold, white snow,
No storm can chill the two-fold glow
    That lights this Happy Birthday!

Then twice the greetings two have known,
With twice the ardor lent to one;
In double measure, doubly done,
    We wish you Happy Birthday!

ELAINE GOODALE.

---

## TRUE RICHES.

SOME little folks went out to tea,
    At 60 Milner Square;
And buns and cake and marmalade
    Adorned the table there.

They sipped their tea from tiny cups
    Of china, white and gold;
And some a *dozen* times were filled,
    So little did they hold.

And Polly put the sugar in,
    And Lucy poured the milk;
And puss sat with them in a chair,
    With skin as soft as silk.

Said Carrie Ritchie, as they laughed
    And talked that happy night,
"You hav'n't seen my necklace yet,
    With golden locket bright.

"I never, all my whole life long,
    Have felt so rich before;
My grandma says she really thinks
    It costs three pounds or more."

"I don't call that so very rich!"
    Tall Kitty Fuller cried;   ·
"I have a handsome diamond ring,
    Aunt left me when she died."

Cried Minnie, "I've a lovely seal
    Of white carnelian, set
In solid gold; but dear papa
    Won't let me wear it yet."

Said laughing Jane, "I've more than all,
    My good luck I may thank:
I think I've nearly twenty pounds
    Within the savings-bank."

Then spoke the lady of the house,
    "Be wealthy as you will,
If you have nothing *more* to boast,
    Ann Gray is richer still."

Amazed, the widow's child they eyed,
    In mourning dress so plain;
Without a trinket in the world
    Of which she might be vain.

"My dears," the lady said (and smiled
    To see sweet Annie start,)
"True riches are not *gems and gold,*
    But *Christ's love in the heart.*"

## MOTHER.

EARLY one summer morning
   I saw two children pass :
Their footsteps, slow yet lightsome,
   Scarce bent the tender grass.

One, lately out of babyhood,
   Looked up with eager eyes :
The other watched her wistfully,
   Oppressed with smothered sighs.

" See, mother ! " cries the little one,
   " I gathered them for you ?
The sweetest flowers and lilies,
   And Mabel has some too."

" Hush, Nellie," whispered Mabel,
   " We have not reached it yet.
Wait till we get there darling,
   It is n't far, my pet."

" Get where ? " asked Nellie. " Tell me,"
   " To the churchyard." Mabel said.
" No, no ! " cried little Nellie,
   And shook her sunny head.

Still Mabel whispered sadly,
   " We must take them to the grave.
Come, darling ? " and the childish voice
   Tried to be clear and brave.

But Nellie still kept calling
  Far up into the blue;
"See, mother, see how pretty!
  We gathered them for you."

And when her sister pleaded,
  She cried — and would not go :—
"Angels don't live in churchyards,
  *My* mother don't, I know!"

Then Mabel bent and kissed her;
  "So be it, dear," she said :
"We'll take them to the arbor,
  And lay them there instead.

"For mother loved it dearly,
  It was the sweetest place!"
And the joy that came to Nellie
  Shone up in Mabel's face.

I saw them turn, and follow
  A path with blossoms bright,
Until the nodding branches
  Concealed them from my sight;

But still like sweetest music
  The words came ringing through;
"See, mother, see, how pretty!
  We gathered them for you."

MARY MAPES DODGE, in St. Nicholas.

# THE DANDELION BOY.

"COME here, my dandelion boy,
    With cheeks so fresh and looks so hale;
I doubt me not but many a toy
    You'll buy with proceeds of your pail.
The kitchen door is yonder, that
    From which the playful kitten ran.
Down, Carlo! Give his head a pat,
    My little dandelion man;

"For surely you are much too brave,
    Thus early struggling for a place
Among the workers, stern and grave,
    Engaged in life's determined race,
For me to call you boy." "Oh, please
    Don't turn them out into the pan,
But so, in handfuls, just like these,"
    Said the little dandelion man.

"What, what! is that the way you do?
    Look at the bottom of the pail!"
Quoth I. "I should not think that you
    Would try to cheat me." Flushed and pale
By turns, his bright face quick became.
    And down his cheeks the hot tears ran:
"I wasn't playing any game,"
    He said — the dandelion man.

"I know I left in here a few ;
    But see! my basket in the street —
I 'll give you half of them, if you
    Won't think that I was trying to cheat."
" But why not give me these ?" quoth I,
    And quick his troubled face did scan,
" And leave those for the next to buy,
    My little dandelion man ?"

An instant he did stand in doubt,
    And then took from his pail, the few
He there had left.   When all were out,
    My eyes sought there to find a clew
For his strange action.   First, some sticks
    . He lifted up, and then his plan
Unfolded, growing quite prolix,—
    The little dandelion man !

" I made a little pen, you see,
    And put these dandelions in,
And violets — I found just three —
    And buttercups for sissy's chin ;
And covered them with sticks — with these —
    To keep 'em fresh for Mary Ann.
I 'll tell you 'bout her, if you please,"
    Said the little dandelion man.

" She 's awful sick, and talks of flowers
    So much, I thought I 'd get her some ;
There ain't none in such streets as ours.
    I thought I 'd best keep kinder mum

'Bout having them, as some folks might
　　Have laughed at me for such a plan,
And called me girl-boy." . . . Ah! quite right,
　　My little dandelion man.

The world is wont to laugh at those,
　　Who seek outside the realms of trade
For joys to palliate earth's woes.
　　A wise man he whose pride has made
A pen of sticks, however rude,
　　To guard from eyes that coldly scan
Soul flowers from its mead and wood,
　　As did my dandelion man.

　　　　　　　EARL MARBLE, in the *Youths' Companion.*

———◆———

## A LESSON.

AS I walked in my garden, one fine summer morn,
　　I noticed a vine growing close by a thorn ;
"Of what use is the briar?" I hastily said,
" Let us take it away, it is worthless and dead."

" Have patience, my dear," said one wiser than I,
" The thorn, although dead, a support will supply
To the frail little vine, lying low on the ground.
Let us lift up its tendrils, and twine them around."

A month or two later, and nothing was seen
Of the thorn, hid beneath its bright mantle of green.
" Convolvulus major," you 'd say was the tree ;
Its bright morning-glories were lovely to see.

Despise not the humble, the aged, the plain;
For nothing is useless, and naught made in vain.
The needful and beautiful grow side by side, —
What God hath united, let not man divide.

C. M. C.

---

## THE GRAY SWAN.

"OH, tell me, sailor, tell me true,
　　Is my little lad, my Elihu,
　　　A-sailing with your ship?"
The sailor's eyes were dim with dew —
"Your little lad, your Elihu?"
　　　　He said, with trembling lip —
　　　　"What little lad? what ship?"

"What little lad? as if there could be
Another such a one as he!
　　　What little lad, do you say?
Why Elihu, who took to the sea
The moment I put him off my knee!
　　　　It was just the other day
　　　　The Gray Swan sailed away."

"The other day?" the sailor's eyes
Stood wide open with surprise —
　　　"The other day? the Swan?"
His heart began in his throat to rise.
"Ay, ay, sir, here in the cupboard lies
　　　　The jacket he had on."
　　　　"And so your lad is gone?"

"Gone with the Swan."  "And did she stand
With her anchor clutching hold of the sand
    For a month, and never stir?"
"Why, to be sure!  I've seen from the land,
Like a lover kissing his lady's hand,
    The wild sea kissing her —
    A sight to remember, sir."


"But, my good mother, do you know
All this was twenty years ago?
    I stood on the Gray Swan's deck,
And to that lad I saw you throw,
Taking it off, as it might be, so,
    The kerchief from your neck."
    "Ay, and he'll bring it back!"


"And did the little lawless lad
That has made you sick, and made you sad,
    Sail with the Gray Swan's crew?"
"Lawless! the man is going mad!
The best boy ever mother had!
    Be sure he sailed with the crew;
    What would you have him do?"


"And he has never written line,
Nor sent you word, nor made you sign
    To say he was alive?"
"Hold! if 't was wrong, the wrong is mine;
Besides, he may be in the brine;
    And could he write from the grave?
    Tut, man! what would you have?"

" Gone twenty years — a long, long cruise !
'T was wicked thus your love to abuse ;
  But if the lad still live,
And come back home, think you, you can
Forgive him ? " " Miserable man,
  You 're mad as the sea — you rave !
  What have I to forgive ? "

The sailor twitched his shirt so blue,
And from within his bosom drew
  The kerchief. She was wild.
" My God ! my Father ! is it true ?
My little lad, my Elihu !
  My blessed boy, my child !
  My dead, my living child ! "

ALICE CARY.

## THE FOX AND THE CAT.

THE fox and the cat, as they travell'd one day,
 With moral discourses cut shorter the way :
" 'T is great," says the Fox, "to make justice our guide !"
" How god-like is mercy !" Grimalkin replied.

Whilst thus they proceeded, a wolf from the wood,
Impatient of hunger, and thirsting for blood,
Rushed forth — as he saw the dull shepherd asleep —
And seized for his victim an innocent sheep.
" In vain, wretched victim, for mercy you bleat ;
When mutton 's at hand," says the wolf, "I must eat."

Grimalkin's astonished!—the Fox stands aghast,
To see the fell beast at his bloody repast.
"What a wretch!" says the cat, "'t is the vilest of brutes.
Does he feed upon flesh, when there's herbage and roots?"
Cries the fox, "While our oaks give us acorns so good,
What a tyrant is this, to spill innocent blood!"

Well, onward they marched, and they moralized still,
Till they came where some poultry picked chaff by a mill.
Sly Reynard surveyed them with gluttonous eyes,
And made, spite of morals, a pullet his prize.
A mouse, too, that chanced from her covert to stray,
The greedy Grimalkin secured as her prey.

A spider, that sat in her web on the wall,
Perceived the poor victims, and pitied their fall;
She said, "Of such murders, how guiltless am I!"
So ran to regale on a new-taken fly.

F. CUNNINGHAM.
*A Garland from the Best Poets,* by Coventry Patmore.

---

## GENTLE WORDS.

USE gentle words, for who can tell
    The blessings they impart?
How oft they fall, as manna falls,
    On some nigh-fainting heart.

In lonely wilds, by light-winged birds,
    Rare seeds have oft been sown,
And hope has sprung from gentle words,
    Where only grief had grown.

ETHEL LYNN BEERS.

## KEEPING HIS WORD.

"ONLY a penny a box," he said;
    But the gentleman turned away his head,
As if he shrank from the wretched sight
Of the boy, who stood in the failing light.

"Oh, sir," he stammered, "you cannot know"—
(And he brushed from his lashes the flakes of snow,
That the sudden tear might have room to fall)
"Or I think,—I think, you would take them all.

"Hungry and cold at our garret pane,
Ruby will watch till I come again,
Bringing the loaf.  The sun has set,
And he has n't a crumb of breakfast as yet.

"One penny, and then I can buy the bread."
The gentleman stopped.  "And you?" he said.
"*I*,—I can bear the hunger and cold;
But Ruby is only five years old.

"I promised our mother, before she went,—
She knew I would do it, and died content—
I promised her, sir, through best, through worst,
I always would think of Ruby first."

The gentleman paused at his open door,
Such tales he had often heard before,
But he fumbled his purse in the twilight drear,
"I have nothing less than a shilling here."

"Oh, sir, if you'll only take the pack,
I'll bring you the change in a moment back.
Indeed you may trust me." "Trust you?—no!
But here is the shilling; take it, and go."

The gentleman lolled in his easy chair,
And the steam from the tea-kettle rose in the air.
He played with his children, and smiled to see
The baby asleep on its mother's knee.

"And now it's nine by the clock," he said,
"Time that my darlings were all a-bed;
Kiss me good-night, and each be sure,
When you're saying your prayers, to remember the poor."

Just then came a message — "A boy at the door;" —
But ere it was uttered, he stood on the floor,
Half breathless, bewildered, and ragged, and strange;
*"I'm Ruby—Mike's brother—I've brought you the change.*

"Mike's hurt, sir! 't was dark; the snow made him blind,
And **he** did n't take notice the train was behind,
Till **he** slipped on the track —and then it whizzed by,
And he's home in the garret —I think he will die.

"Yet nothing would quiet him, sir, — nothing would do,
But out through the snow I must hurry to you.
Of his hurt, he was certain you would not have heard,
And so you might think *he had broken his word.*"

When the garret they hastily entered, they saw,
Two arms, bruised and bleeding, outstretched on the straw,
*"You did it, dear Ruby? God bless you!"* he said;
And the boy, gladly smiling, sank back — and was dead.

# BEAUTIFUL HANDS.

SUCH beautiful, beautiful hands!
  They're neither white nor small;
And you, I know, would scarcely think
  That they were fair at all.
I've looked on hands, whose form and hue
  A sculptor's dream might be;
Yet are these aged, wrinkled hands
  Most beautiful to me.

Such beautiful, beautiful hands!
  Though heart were weary and sad,
These patient hands kept toiling on,
  That the children might be glad.
I almost weep, as, looking back
  To childhood's distant day,
I think how these hands rested not,
  When mine were at their play.

Such beautiful, beautiful hands!
  They're growing feeble now;
For time and pain have left their work
  On hand and heart and brow.
Alas! alas! the nearing time,
  And the sad, sad day to me,
When 'neath the daisies, out of sight,
  These hands will folded be.

But, oh! beyond this shadow-lamp,
  Where all is bright and fair,
I know full well these dear old hands
  Will palms of victory bear.
Where crystal streams, through endless years,
  Flow over golden sands,
And where the old grow young again,
  I'll clasp my mother's hands.

Ellen M. H. Gates.

## BEAUTY.

BEAUTIFUL faces they, that wear
  The light of a pleasant spirit there,
It matters little if dark or fair.

Beautiful hands are they, that do
The works of the noble, good, and true,
Busy for them the long day through.

Beautiful feet are they, that go,
Swiftly to lighten another's woe,
Through summer's heat and winter's snow.

Beautiful children, if rich or poor,
Who walk the pathways sweet and pure,
That lead to the mansions strong and sure.

Beautiful they, who from every land
Hasten to join the blood-washed band,
Who shall shine in glory at Christ's right hand.

# NOT ONE TO SPARE.

"WHICH shall it be?" "Which shall it be?"
    I looked at John — John looked at me,
(Dear patient John, who loves me yet,
As well as though my locks were jet ;)
And when I found that I must speak,
My voice seemed strangely low and weak.
"Tell me again what Robert said !"
And then I, listening, bent my head.
"This is his letter : 'I will give
A house and land while you shall live,
If, in return, from out your seven,
One child to me for aye is given.'"
I looked at John's old garments worn ;
I thought of all that John had borne
Of poverty, and work, and care,
Which I, though willing, could not share ;
I thought of seven mouths to feed,
Of seven little children's need,
And then of this, — "Come, John," said I,
"We 'll choose among them as they lie
Asleep ;" so, walking hand in hand,
Dear John and I surveyed our band.
First to the cradle lightly stepped,
Where Lilian, the baby, slept,
A glory 'gainst the pillow white.
Softly the father stooped to lay
His rough hand down in loving way,

When dream or whisper made her stir,
And huskily he said, "Not her."
We stopped beside the trundle-bed,
And, one long ray of lamplight shed
Athwart the boyish faces there,
In sleep so pitiful and fair.
I saw on Jamie's rough, red cheek
A tear undried.  Ere John could speak,
"He's but a baby, too," said I,
And kissed him as we hurried by.
Pale, patient Robbie's angel face
Still in his sleep bore suffering's trace.
"No, for a thousand crowns, not him,"
He whispered, while our eyes were dim.
Poor Dick! bad Dick! our wayward son,
Turbulent, reckless, idle one,—
Could he be spared?  "Nay, He who gave
Bid us befriend him to his grave.
Only a mother's heart can be
Patient enough for such as he ;
And so," said John, "I would not dare
To send him from her bedside prayer."
Then stole we softly up above,
And knelt by Mary, child of love.
"Perhaps for her 't would better be,"
I said to John.  Quite silently
He lifted up a curl, that lay
Across her cheek in wilful way,
And shook his head, "Nay, love, not thee."
The while my heart beat audibly.
Only one more, our eldest lad,
Trusty and truthful, good and glad,—

So like his father. "No, John, no;
I cannot, will not, let him go."
And so he wrote, in courteous way,
We could not drive one child away;
And afterward toil lighter seemed,
Thinking of that of which we dreamed,
Happy in truth, that not one face
Was missed from its accustomed place;
Thankful to work for all the seven,
Trusting the rest to One in heaven!

———◆———

## MUFF AND TUFF.

"A STORY! yes, a story! we've caught you, aunty dear!
This window-seat is just the place, it is so cosy
here.
Now please don't let the 'curtain drop,' or say 'I came
away,'
In just the very nicest part, as 't was the other day."

"Well, listen then, 'Once on a time,' — I know *that* suits
you well,
There lived two cunning little mice, in cottage 'Shady
Dell,'
With naught to do, the livelong day, but scamper round
and eat
The dainty bits of cake and pie, then wash their little
feet.

"In Shady Dell, there also lived, two little maidens small,
Just full of fun and frolic.   Each had a lovely doll;
And with those dolls they played keep house, and neatly
    spread each meal,
With cloth so white, with silver bright, and cups of orange
    peel.

"Unknown to them, these little mice were glad to copy
    all
The pretty ways, and merry plays, they watched from out
    the wall.
They found a cunning little block, and scorned to use it
    bare,
But hastened to the bureau-drawer, for pretty kerchief
    there.

"They spread this dainty table-cloth, and then began to
    cry,
'Oh, where shall we find dishes, too, just fit for us? Oh
    my!
We'll have to use these tiny chips, — well, many such
    I've seen,
With just a streak of paint, bright yellow, red, and green,

"And placed upon the parlor walls, and praised as 'very
    nice;'
So I am sure they'll do for plates, for two such little
    mice.
This plate of tin will do for bread, this larger one for
    cheese;
Do shut that door, pray, dearest Tuff, or you will make
    me sneeze.

"Their dinner o'er, each took a nap, then wakened with
      a start;
To make their house quite neat and clean, each did his
      little part:
Tuff once more flew to bureau drawer, for bag to hold
      the crumbs,
He found some nice kid mittens there, and took away the
      thumbs.

"'I know, dear Muff, they're for that use, and so I made
      no muss;
They smell so strong of cake, dear Milly placed them
      there for us.
I found a pretty feather, too, not needed on her hat."
With this, they swept the floor quite clean, and then
      shook out the mat.

"Then peeping out from little hole, they heard Kate's
      mother say,
'That mouse has cut these mitts so well, I'll pay him
      right away,
And give him something very nice, he'll nibble at it quick;
I'll cut a piece from out this cheese, in shape just like a
      brick.'

"So merry game of hide and seek, these little mice did take,
Then down the nursery stairs in haste, their frisky way
      did make.
Milly and Kate were fast asleep, but just there on the
      floor,
They spied the prettiest little house, with round, wide
      open door;

"And shining scraper, too, so like the grand one down
  below,
For use in muddy weather, or when there falls a snow.
Within each door, upon a peg, there hung a generous
  slice
Of toasted cheese, the very best that ever tempted mice.

"'I smell a treat,' said little Muff, and puckered up his
  nose ;
'I smell a treat,' said little Tuff, and scampered on his
  toes.
''Tis all for us! 'tis all for us! did we not hear them say,
We'd worked so well, so very well, that we should have
  our pay?'

"''Tis toasted cheese!' said little Muff, and touched some
  with his nose ;
''Tis toasted cheese!' said little Tuff, and hit some with
  his toes ;
Alas! alas! their race was run, the shining scrapers slipped,
And all their plans for future joys, within the bud were
  nipped."

I paused for breath, and stole a kiss, but not a word was
  said
By any little girl or boy ; quite hushed each curly head.
I drew them close, so sad they were, for babes of tender
  years !
I found each eye, brown, black, and blue, was blinded by
  their tears.

Jenny Wallis.

# THE LITTLE CLAM.

WHEN the merry little waves come racing, chasing in
    from sea,
Seeing which can run the fastest, laughing loudly in their
    glee,
I wonder if they ever think what joy their voices bring
To the little clam, as snug at home he hears them shout
    and sing?
        Oh, the happy little clam!
        Oh, the jolly little clam!
        Oh, the merry little clam!
        When the tide comes in from sea.

But when the waves are weary, playing tag upon the shore,
And run away as quickly as they hastened in before,
Oh, then the little clam sheds tears, salt tears of bitter
    woe ;
For well he knows what danger comes, whene'er the tide
    is low.
        Oh, the doleful little clam!
        Oh, the long-faced little clam!
        Oh, the tearful little clam!
        When he knows the tide is low.

His house is strong, and all about him are walls of mud
    and sand,
Which shut him in quite safe and sound, (I hope you
    understand.)

He never feels the snow and ice; for, sheltered close and
    warm,
He rests within his shell, nor minds the pelting winter
    storm.
        Oh, the sheltered little clam!
        Oh, the comfortable clam!
        Oh, the muddy little clam!
        Through the pelting winter storm.


But spring and summer come, when every little girl and
    boy
Think "clamming" just the nicest part, of all their daily
    joy;
Oh, then the little clam shrinks up, with terror and with
    fears,
And over him at dead low tide, an awful sound he hears.
        Oh, the wretched little clam!
        Oh, the frightened little clam!
        Oh, the squirming little clam!
        When that awful sound he hears.


Still nearer, and more near it comes. Alas! what shall
    he do?
He has no legs to run away, he cannot walk like you;
So, shivering with agony, he crouches in his shell.
His dreadful terror and suspense, no human tongue can
    tell.
        Oh, the terror-stricken clam!
        Oh, the hunted little clam!
        Oh, the legless little clam!
        As he shrinks within his shell.

At last the awful moment comes, when, just outside his door,
He hears the thumping of the spades, and then he knows
      no more,
Till, torn from home and happiness, he wakens by and by,
To find himself in cracker-crumbs, all ready for a fry.
      Oh, the helpless little clam!
      Oh, the finished little clam!
      Oh, the thoughts which fill that clam
      As he sizzles in the fry!

Now, when you hear that any one is "happy as a clam,"
Remember that clam-life, like yours, is not all cake and jam.
There are two sides to everything, high tide as well as low;
And clams, like children, have their ups and downs, their
      ebb and flow.
      Think kindly of the clam!
      The happy little clam!
      And don't forget the clam,
      Whene'er the tide is low.

---

## THE TRUE STORY OF LITTLE BOY BLUE.

LITTLE Boy Blue, so the story goes,
   One morning, while reading, fell fast asleep,
When he should have been, as every one knows,
   Watching the cows and sheep.

All of you children remember, what
   Came of the nap on that summer morn, —
How the sheep got into the meadow lot
   The cows got into the corn.

Neglecting a duty is wrong, of course,
    But I always felt, if we could know,
That the matter was made a great deal worse
    Than it should have been; and so

I find, in my sifting, that there was one
    More to blame than Little Boy Blue.
I'm anxious to have full justice done,
    And so, I know, are you.

The one to blame I have found to be,
    I'm sorry to say it, Little Bo-Peep;
But you will remember, perhaps, that she
    Had trouble about her sheep.

Well, Little Bo-Peep came tripping along,
    The sheep she tended were running at large;
Little Boy Blue sat singing a song,
    Faithfully minding his charge.

Said Little Bo-Peep, "It's a burning shame
    That you should sit here from week to week;
Just leave your work, and we'll play a game,
    Oh,—well, of hide and go seek."

It was dull work, and he liked to play
    Better, I'm sure, than to eat or sleep;
He liked the bloom of the summer day,
    He liked—he liked Bo-Peep.

And so, with many a laugh and shout,
    They hid from each other, now here, now there;
And, whether the cows were in or out,
    Bo-Peep had never a care.

"I will hide once more," said the little maid;
  "You shall not find me this time, I say.
Shut your eyes up tight" — (Boy Blue obeyed,)
  "Under this stack of hay.

"Now wait till I call," said Miss Bo-Peep;
  And over the meadows she slipped away,
With never a thought for cows or sheep —
  Alas, alas, the day!

And long and patiently waited he,
  For the blithesome call from her rosy lip.
He waited in vain, — quite like, you see,
  The boy on the burning ship.

She let down the bars, did Miss Bo-Peep, —
  Such trifles as bars she held in scorn, —
And into the meadows went the sheep,
  And the cows went into the corn.

By and by, when they found Boy Blue,
  *In the merest doze*, he took the blame.
It was very fine, I think, don't you,
  Not to mention Bo-Peep's name?

Thus it has happened, that all these years
  He has borne the blame she ought to share.
Since I know the truth of it, it appears
  To me to be only fair

To tell the story, from shore to shore,
  From sea to sea, and from sun to sun;
Because I think, as I said before,
  I like to see justice done.

And whatever you 've read or seen or heard,
　Believe me, children, I tell the true
And only genuine, (take my word,)
　Story of Little Boy Blue.

CARLOTTA PERRY, in *The Independent.*

---

## THE RED BREAST OF THE ROBIN.

### AN IRISH LEGEND.

OF all the merry little birds, that live up in the tree,
　And carol from the sycamore and chestnut,
The prettiest little gentleman, that dearest is to me,
　Is the one in coat of brown, and scarlet waistcoat.
　　　　It 's cockit little robin,
　　　　And his head he keeps a bobbin'.
Of all the other pretty birdies I 'd choose him ;
　　　　For he sings so sweetly still
　　　　Through his tiny, slender bill,
With a little patch of red upon his bosom.

When the frost is in the air, and the snow upon the ground,
　To the other little birdies so bewilderin',
Picking up the crumbs, near the window he is found,
　Singing Christmas stories to the children :
　　　　Of how two tender babes
　　　　Were left in woodland glades,
By a cruel man, who took 'em there to lose 'em :
　　　　But Bobby saw the crime,
　　　　(He was watching all the time.)
And he blushed a perfect crimson on his bosom.

When the changing leaves of autumn around us thickly
    fall,
  And everything seems sorrowful and saddening,
Robin may be heard on the corner of a wall,
  Singing what is solacing and gladdening;
        And sure, from what I've heard,
        He's God's own little bird,
And sings to those in sorrow, just to amuse 'em;
        But once he sat forlorn,
        On a cruel Crown of Thorn,
And the blood it stained his pretty little bosom.

———◆———

## NOSE AND EYES.

BETWEEN Nose and Eyes a strange contest arose,—
  The spectacles set them unhappily wrong.
The point in dispute was, as all the world knows,
  To which the said spectacles ought to belong.

So the Tongue was the lawyer, and argued the cause
  With a great deal of skill, and a wig full of learning;
While Chief Baron Ear sat to balance the laws,
  So famed for his talent in nicely discerning.

"In behalf of the Nose, it will quickly appear,
  And your lordship," he said, "will undoubtedly find,
That the Nose has had spectacles always in wear,
  Which amounts to possession time out of mind."

Then, holding the spectacles up to the court,—
  "Your lordship observes, they are made with a straddle
As wide as the ridge of the Nose is, in short,
  Designed to sit close to it, just like a saddle.

"Again, would your lordship a moment suppose,
  ('T is a case that has happened, and may be again,)
That the visage or countenance had not a nose,
  Pray who would, or who could wear spectacles then?

"On the whole it appears, and my argument shows,
  With a reasoning the court will never condemn,
That the spectacles plainly were made for the Nose,
  And the Nose was as plainly intended for them."

Then, shifting his side, as a lawyer knows how,
  He pleaded again in behalf of the Eyes:
But what were his arguments few people know,
  For the court did not think them equally wise.

So his lordship decreed, with a grave, solemn tone,
  Decisive and clear, without one if or but,
That whenever the Nose put the spectacles on,
  By daylight or candlelight, Eyes should be shut.

                                        COWPER

---

## THE FLIGHT OF THE BIRDS.

O WISE little birds, how do you know
    The way to go
Southward and northward, to and fro?
Far up in the ether piped they:

"We but obey
One that calleth us, far away.
He calleth, and calleth, year by year,
 Now there, now here;
Ever he maketh the way appear."
Dear little birds, He calleth me,
 Who calleth thee.
Would that I might as trusting be.

HARRIET McEWEN KIMBALL, in Scribner's Monthly.

—◆—

## THE RATTLE OF THE BONES.

HOW many bones in the human face?
 Fourteen, when they're all in place.

How many bones in the human head?
Eight, my child, as I've often said.

How many bones in the human ear?
Four in each, and they help to hear.

How many bones in the human spine?
Twenty-four, like a climbing vine.

How many bones in the human chest?
Twenty-four ribs, and two of the rest.

How many bones the shoulders bind?
Two in each — one before, one behind.

How many bones in the human arm?
In each arm one; two in each forearm.

How many bones in the human wrist?
Eight in each, if none are missed.

How many bones in the palm of the hand?
Five in each, with many a band.

How many bones in the fingers ten?
Twenty-eight, and by joints they bend.

How many bones in human hip?
One in each; like a dish they dip.

How many bones in the human thigh?
One in each, and deep they lie.

How many bones in the human knees?
One in each, the kneepan, please.

How many bones in the leg from the knee?
Two in each, we can plainly see.

How many bones in the ankle strong?
Seven in each, but none are long.

How many bones in the ball of the foot?
Five in each, as the palms were put.

How many bones in the toes, half a score?
Twenty-eight, and there are no more.

And now all together, these many bones wait,
And they count, in a body, two hundred and eight.

And then we have, in the human mouth,
Of upper and under, thirty-two teeth.

And now and then have a bone, I should think,
That forms on a joint, or to fill up a chink,—

A Sesamoid bone, or a Wormian, we call;
And now we may rest, for we've told them all.

*Indianapolis Sentinel.*

---

## THE GRUMBLER.

### HIS YOUTH.

HIS cap was too thick, and his coat was too thin;
    He couldn't be quiet; he hated a din;
He hated to write, and he hated to read;
He was certainly very much injured indeed!
He must study and toil over work he detested;
His parents were strict; and he never was rested;
He knew he was wretched as wretched could be,
There was no one so wretchedly wretched as he.

### HIS MATURITY.

His farm was too small, and his taxes too big:
He was selfish and lazy, and cross as a pig;
His wife was too silly, his children too rude,
And just because he was uncommonly good!

He had n't got money enough and to spare ;
He had nothing at all fit to eat or to wear ;
He knew he was wretched as wretched could be,
There was no one so wretchedly wretched as he !

### HIS OLD AGE.

He finds he has sorrows more deep than his fears ;
He grumbles to think he has grumbled for years ;
He grumbles to think he has grumbled away
His home and his children, his life's little day ;
But alas ! 't is too late ! it is no use to say
That his eyes are too dim, and his hair is too gray ;
He knows he is wretched as wretched can be,
There *is* no one so wretchedly wretched as he !

DORA READ GOODALE.

---

## LITTLE PAT AND THE PARSON.

HE stands at the door of the church, peeping in,
    No troublesome beadle is near him ;
The preacher is talking of sinners and sin,
    And little Pat trembles to hear him ;

A poor little fellow, alone and forlorn,
    Who never knew parent, or duty ;
His head is uncovered, his jacket is torn,
    And hunger has withered his beauty.

The white-headed gentleman shut in the box,
    Seems growing more angry each minute ;
He doubles his fist, and the cushion he knocks,
    As if anxious to know what is in it.

He scolds at the people who sit in the pews,—
    Pat takes them for kings and princesses;
(With his little bare feet, he delights in their shoes;
    In his rags, he feels proud of their dresses!)


The parson exhorts them to think of their need,
    To turn from the world's dissipation,
The naked to clothe, and the hungry to feed,—
    Pat listens with strong approbation!


And, when the old clergyman walks down the aisle,
    Pat runs up to meet him right gladly;
"Sure, give me my dinner!" says he, with a smile,
    "And a jacket; I want them quite badly."


The kings and princesses indignantly stare,
    The beadle gets word of the danger,
And, shaking his silver-tipped stick in the air,
    Looks knives at the poor little stranger.


But Pat's not afraid, he is sparkling with joy,
    And cries — who so willing to cry it?—
"You'll give me my dinner — I'm such a poor boy;
    You said so,— now don't you deny it."


The pompous old beadle may grumble and glare,
    And growl about robbers and arson;
But the boy who has faith in the sermon stands there,
    And smiles at the white-headed parson!

The kings and princesses may wonder and frown,
   And whisper he wants better teaching;
But the white-headed parson looks tenderly down
   On the boy who has faith in his preaching.

He takes him away without question or blame,
   As eager as Patsy, to press on ;
For he thinks a good dinner, (and Pat thinks the same),
   Is the moral that lies in the lesson.

And after long years, when Pat, handsomely dressed,—
   A smart footman,— is asked to determine,
Of all earthly things, what's the thing he likes best,
   He says, "Och! shure, the master's ould sermin!"

From Poems Written for a Child.

## THE OPEN DOOR.

WITHIN a town of Holland, once
      A widow dwelt, 't is said,
So poor, alas! her children asked,
      One night, in vain, for bread.
But this poor woman loved the Lord,
      And knew that he was good ;
So, with her little ones around,
      She prayed to him for food.

When prayer was done, the eldest child,
      A boy of eight years old,
Said softly, "In the Holy Book,
      Dear mother, we are told

How God, with food by ravens brought,
    Supplied His Prophet's need."
" Yes," answered she, " but that, my son,
    Was long ago, indeed."


" But, mother, God may do again,
    What he has done before ;
And so, to let the bird fly in,
    I will unclose the door."
Then little Dirk, in simple faith,
    Threw ope the door full wide,
So that the radiance of their lamp
    Fell on the path outside.


Ere long, the burgomaster passed,
    And, noticing the light,
Paused to inquire why thus the door
    Was open so at night.
" My little Dirk has done it, sir,"
    The widow, smiling, said,
" That ravens might fly in and bring
    My hungry children bread."


" Indeed ! " the burgomaster cried,
    " Then here 's a raven, lad ;
Come to my home and you shall see
    Where bread may soon be had."
Along the street, to his own house,
    He quickly led the boy,
And sent him back with food that filled
    His humble home with joy.

The supper ended, little Dirk
    Went to the open door,
Looked up, and said, " We thank thee, Lord,"
    Then shut it fast once more.
For though no bird had entered in,
    He knew that God, on high,
Had hearkened to his mother's prayer,
    And sent this full supply.

———◆———

## AN OLD CHRISTMAS RHYME.

THE first day of Christmas, my true love, he
      Brought unto me,
Part of a bough of a juniper tree.

The second day of Christmas, my true love, he
      Brought unto me,
Two French hens, and part of a bough of a juniper tree.

The third day of Christmas, my true love, he
      Brought unto me,
Three tole of birds, two French hens, and part of a bough
    of a juniper tree.

The fourth day of Christmas, my true love, he
      Brought unto me,
Four turtle-doves, three tole of birds, two French hens,
    and part of a bough of a juniper tree.

The fifth day of Christmas, my true love, he
      Brought unto me,
Five gold rings, four turtle-doves, three tole of birds, two
    French hens, and part of a bough of a juniper tree.

The sixth day of Christmas, my true love, he
        Brought unto me,
Six geese a-laying, five gold rings, four turtle-doves, three
    tole of birds, two French hens, and part of a bough
    of a juniper tree.

The seventh day of Christmas, my true love, he
        Brought unto me,
Seven swans a-swimming, six geese a-laying, five gold
    rings, four turtle-doves, three tole of birds, two
    French hens, and part of a bough of a juniper tree.

The eighth day of Christmas, my true love, he
        Brought unto me,
Eight ladies dancing, seven swans a-swimming, six geese
    a-laying, five gold rings, four turtle-doves, three tole
    of birds, two French hens, and part of a bough of
    a juniper tree.

The ninth day of Christmas, my true love, he
        Brought unto me,
Nine lords a-piping, eight ladies dancing, seven swans a-
    swimming, six geese a-laying, five gold rings, four
    turtle-doves, three tole of birds, two French hens,
    and part of a bough of a juniper tree.

The tenth day of Christmas, my true love, he
        Brought unto me,
Ten drums a-beating, nine lords a-piping, eight ladies dan-
    cing, seven swans a-swimming, six geese a-laying,
    five gold rings, four turtle-doves, three tole of birds,
    two French hens, and part of a bough of a juniper
    tree.

The eleventh day of Christmas, my true love, he
      Brought unto me,
Eleven logs a-burning, ten drums a-beating, nine lords a-
    piping, eight ladies dancing, seven swans a-swimming,
    six geese a-laying, five gold rings, four turtle-doves,
    three tole of birds, two French hens, and part of a
    bough of a juniper tree.

The twelfth day of Christmas, my true love, he
      Brought unto me,
Twelve bowls a-foaming, eleven logs a-burning, ten drums
    a-beating, nine lords a-piping, eight ladies dancing,
    seven swans a-swimming, six geese a-laying, five gold
    rings, four turtle-doves, three tole of birds, two
    French hens, and part of a bough of a juniper tree.

---

## THE PET GREYHOUND.

I'M a pretty little greyhound,
    Of faultless pedigree ;
I cost a pile of money,
    Which was gladly paid for me.

Although 't is wintry weather,
    My coat is very thin ;
So, while other dogs are roaming,
    I prudently stay in.

I am so very slender,
    That you would never guess
What I can eat for dinner,
    A bushel — more or less.

First, comes a plate of turkey,
　　Or other kind of meat ;
But I have only just begun,
　　So let me keep my seat.

Now follow sticks of celery,
　　Then juicy apple slice ;
Then dainty bits of cake and cheese,
　　And nuts, that are so nice.

I love my master dearly,
　　Although I am so small,
And when I hear his whistle,
　　I run out in the hall,

And then I bark so loudly,
　　That when he opes the door,
He 's sure to see me quickly,
　　A dancing round the floor.

And then I feel so happy,
　　I jump up in his face ;
And wag my tail so proudly,
　　They say — with perfect grace.

Now, if you see dear Bertha,
　　I wish that you would tell her,
That this is the *true* story,
　　Of little Tony Weller.

JENNIE WALLIS.

## THE VASE AND THE PITCHER.

### A FABLE.

ONE day, when a grand entertainment was ended,
A rich China Vase, lately come from abroad,
In which every tint of the rainbow was blended,
Spoke thus, to a Pitcher, that stood on the board.

"I hope, rustic neighbor, you don't feel distressed,
At standing before me, so shabbily dressed;
It will mitigate, maybe, your feelings, to know,
That though so superb, I can stoop to the low.

"'T is true, that before I came from abroad,
Beyond the wide Ganges, I lived with a lord;
'T is true, in the west, no king can procure
For his service of state, so splendid a ewer.

"'T is true, that gay ladies, in feathers and pearls,
Survey and admire me,— and barons and earls;
'T is true, that I am, as you must understand,
Prodigiously rich, and excessively grand.

" But you, paltry bottle! I pity your fate:
Whence came ye, coarse neighbor, I prithee relate,
And tell us, how is it you ever endure
So graceless a shape, and so vile a contour?"

The Pitcher, who stood with his hand on his hip,
Shrugged up his round shoulders, and curled his brown lip,
And, grave to appearance, but laughing inside,
He thus, from his orifice, coldly replied:

"I come, noble Vase, from the cottage below,
Where I serve a poor husbandman, if you must know;
And my trade (might I venture to name such a thing)
Is, bringing pure water each morn from the spring.

"There's a notable lass, who at dawn of the day,
When the dew-drops yet glisten on meadow and spray,
When the lark soars aloft, and the breezes are cool,
Sets off, on light tiptoe, with me, to the pool.

"The pool is surrounded with willow and ash;
At noon, in the sun, its dark waters will flash;
And through the deep shade, you at intervals hear,
The lowing of kine, in the meadow-land near.

"The sheep with their lambkins there browse at their ease,
Beneath the cool arch of embowering trees;
While low creeping herbs give their sweets to the air,
Wild thyme, and the violet, and primroses fair.

"'T is here, that myself, every morning she bears;
Then back to the cot in the valley repairs;
The fagot is blazing, the breakfast is placed,
And appetite sweetens coarse fare to the taste.

"In these humble services, passes my life,
Remote from the city — its noise, and its strife;
Though homely, I'm fit for the work of the day,
And I am not ashamed of my true British clay.

"And now, noble Vase, may I ask if 't is true,
That you stand here every day, with nothing to do?
A poor idle gentleman, up in your niche,
Quite useless; — and nothing but handsome and rich?

"They neither entrust you with victuals nor drink;
You must have but a poor, sorry life on 't, I think;
And though such an elegant creature you're thought,
Pray are you not tired, with doing of nought?

But the Vase would not answer such questions as these;
And the Pitcher felt glad he was not a Chinese.

JANE TAYLOR.

——◆——

## QUEEN FLORA'S CHOIR.

'TWAS a month before Easter, and through the cold
    ground,
Not a flower was stirring, not a bud to be found;
But covered all close, in their warm, cosy bed,
Each drowsily slept, nor lifted a head.
The birds had all met for their spring jubilee,
And the woods gaily rang, with their musical glee;
The trees whispered low, with a glad, knowing air,
Their hopes that Queen Flora now soon would be there.

And sure enough, soon from the far southern land
Came the sweet, floating sounds of a fairy-like band ·
A tiny brass horn, and a little bass drum,
With a shrill little fife, told that Flora had come.
A blue-bottle fly made the horn "fairly hum;"
A fat bumble-bee beat the little bass drum;
While a lively young cricket performed on the fife,
Making music as sweet as e'er heard in your life.

And now came the car, where, sweetly serene,
On an emerald throne sat the flowers' fair queen:
Two humming-birds drew her, — two dainty, bright things,
That looked, when they moved, like a rainbow on wings.
As onward they came, with a soft southern breeze,
She nodded and smiled to the low-bowing trees;
But vainly she looked for a welcoming flower,
And her voice rang out clear, with a magical power:

"Up, crocus, up, snow-drop, up, cowslip and daisy;
Up, violet blue! What makes you so lazy?
The sweet Easter chimes now soon will be heard,
The glad matin-bells of the new-wakened world."
Then each little bud that loves early to rise,
Threw back the warm cover, and opened her eyes;
And one little crocus, than others more bold,
Stuck out a green finger to see if 't were cold.

"Oh, sisters," she said, "Queen Flora has come,
Don't you hear the brass horn, and splendid bass drum?
She is calling us, now, our voices to raise,
To be ready to join in the sweet Easter praise."
And soon they were out, in garments arrayed,
That good mother earth had secretly made,
Awakening all sluggards with wee trumpet call,
And greeting old friends with a "Good-morning, all!"

Queen Flora passed on; and, joining her train,
The flowers sprang up over meadow and plain;
The little brass band growing louder and clear,
Till all the great world seemed pausing to hear.

And what was the hymn that waked with the dawn,
Thrilling heaven and earth on the fair Easter morn?
'T was a hymn of grand praise from Flora's full choir,
To the great God above, rising higher and higher,
Till angels, enraptured, caught up the glad strain,
And echoed it back from their harp-strings again.

Lee Rouseau, in *The Churchman.*

---

## FROST.

THE Frost looked forth, one still, clear night,
   And he said, " Now I shall be out of sight;
So through the valley, and over the height,
     In silence I 'll take my way;
I will not go on like that blustering train,
The wind and the snow, the hail and the rain,
Who make so much bustle and noise in vain,
     But I 'll be as busy as they!"

Then he went to the mountain and powdered its crest;
He climbed up the trees and their boughs he dressed
With diamonds and pearls, and over the breast
     Of the quivering lake, he spread
A coat of mail, that it need not fear
The downward point of many a spear,
That he hung on its margin, far and near,
     Where a rock could rear its head.

He went to the windows of those who slept,
And over each pane like a fairy crept;
Wherever he breathed, wherever he stepped,

By the light of the moon, were seen
Most beautiful things.  There were flowers and trees,
There were bevies of birds, and swarms of bees, —
There were cities, thrones, temples and towers! and these
All pictured in silver sheen!

But he did one thing that was hardly fair;
He went to the cupboard, and finding there
That all had forgotten for him to prepare,
"Now just to set them thinking,
I 'll bite this basket of fruit," said he;
"This bloated pitcher I 'll burst in three!
And the glass of water they 've left for me,
Shall 'tchick,' to tell them I 'm drinking!"

H. F. Gould

———◆———

## OUR GYPSY.

OUR little pet dog, whose name was Gyp,
Was anxious to travel, and gave us the slip,
So gay and so happy, he quitted the house,
Without giving a warning, or telling a mouse.
"The world owes me a living," he cheerily thought,
"And the best of experience, they say must be bought.
I have looked out my window for many a day,
And longed with my comrades to gambol and play;
No stick in the corner can terrify me,
Can a gypsy be happy unless he is free?
I 'll run round the corner on a gay little lark,
For no one will see me, 't is growing so dark."

He rounded "Goat Corner" on his four little feet,
He scattered the geese, and he dashed up the street.
He went to the butcher's his supper to beg,
Of a nice little lamb he asked but the leg;
But the butcher quite furiously stamped on the floor,
And forbade him again to darken his door.
Alas for poor Gypsy! his courage soon fled,
As, tired and hungry, he sought for his bed;
But his soft woollen shawl could nowhere be found,
And, weary with running, he slept on the ground.
Next morning, he started in search of a bone,
But all he received was a three-cornered stone,
Which a bad boy threw at his poor little back,
And then with a stick, he hit him a crack.
He carried him home, half dead with fright,
Though he struggled and kicked, with all his might.
He was tied to a post by his little red collar,
And offered for sale for only one dollar.
He struggled, he whined, he curled in his tail;
He cried to go home, but none heeded his wail.
Relief came at last, for his head it grew smaller,
Until he easily slipped from his collar;
When no one was looking, he hied to the street,
And soon trotted home on those four little feet;
A sad little prodigal, he barked at the door:
"Oh, let me come in, I will wander no more;
Oh, pity my sorrows, please give me some meat,
I've had none for so long, 't will be a great treat."
Not long was he standing outside at the door,
For soon he was dancing inside, on the floor.
A mug of milk and a plate of meat
Soon made his happiness complete.

A splendid wash and a rubbing down,
Now, he's the handsomest dog in town.
Dear little Gypsy now has a new collar;
Sweet little Gypsy is bright as a dollar;
He knows what it is to live in the street,
And gladly he stays where there's plenty to eat.

JENNY WALLIS.

## A PLEASANT SATURDAY NIGHT.

HOW pleasant is Saturday night,
    When I've tried all the week to be good ·
Not spoken a word that was bad,
    And obliged every one that I could.

To-morrow, the holy day comes,
    Which our merciful Father has given;
That we may have rest from our toil,
    And prepare for the joys of his heaven.

## THE FOX AND THE HEN.

A WHITE old hen, with yellow legs,
    Who'd laid her master many eggs,
Which, from her nest, the boys had taken,
To put in cake or fry with bacon,
Was roosting in an outer hovel,
Where barrel, bird-cage, riddle, shovel,
Tub, piggin, corn-bag, all together,
Were put to keep them from the weather;

When an old fox stole in one night,
As the full moon was shining bright,
Hoping, if he his nose might stick in,
That he might carry off a chicken, —
Or, from the window, ledge, or shelf,
Might jump, — and reach the old hen herself.
Her roost, however, was so high,
He found it was in vain to try
By all his jumping, to get at her,
So, then, said he, "I think I 'll flatter
The old fool's vanity, for look!
Have her, I must, by hook or crook.
In fact, I 've thought so much about her,
That I should fare very ill without her."
So thus, — spake Reynard, smooth and sly,
And thus, — Dame Partlett made reply.

*R.*     Good evening, madame, how d 'ye do?
*D. P.*  I 'm none the better, sir, for you.
*R.*     Better, you need not, cannot be,
         You 're always well enough for me.
*D. P.*  Well, if I am then, as you own,
         Pray sir, let well enough, alone.
*R.*     Indeed, dear madame, that hath taught me
         To care for you, and that hath brought me
         Thus late to call, perhaps 't is rude,
         But, ma'am, I hope I don't intrude.
*D. P.*  Intrude! indeed, sir, but you do!
*R.*     It grieves me to hear that from you,
         I 'll therefore say no more at present
         Than just to hint, that as it 's pleasant,
         I 've called to invite you to a walk.

*D. P.*   A walk! the like who ever heard?
       A quadruped, to woo a bird?
       I'm sick, and early went to bed,
       And scarcely can hold up my head.

*R.*      Sick! my dear lady, what can ail?
       Indeed, you do look very pale,
       I'm sure your illness can arise
       But from the want of exercise;
       Too much confinement fades the fair,
       A pleasant walk in open air,
       With pleasant company at night,
       When the moon shines, will set all right,
       And, should you tire, I'll call a hack,
       Or, better, take you on my back.
       I'm sure, tho' I don't mean to flatter,
       That one of us will be the fatter
       For such a walk; nay, never fear
       The jealousy of chanticleer,
       He shall not harm a single feather
       Of your fair neck, while we're together.
       Your neck, — aye, now I think upon it,
       With your white shawl and scarlet bonnet,
       You'll be by all, both far and near,
       Mistaken for a cherub, dear.

*D. P.*   Well, Mr. Reynard, are you done?
       If so, I think you'd better run;
       My master's coming to the hovel;
       You see that broom-stick, and that shovel,
       You see that door that you came in at,
       And if you're not off in half a minute,
       Instead of fowls, or even a chicken,
       You'll get what you deserve, a kicking.

The wily flatterer dropped his chin,
And out he sneaked, as he sneaked in.

### MORAL.

The cunning, seldom gain their ends,
The wise, are never without friends.

———◆———

## THREE LITTLE GRAVES.

'TWAS Autumn, and the leaves were dry,
   And rustling on the ground,
The chilly wind went whistling by,
   With low and pensive sound;

As through the graveyard's lone retreat,
   By meditation led,
I walked with slow and cautious feet,
   Above the sleeping dead.

Three little graves, ranged side by side,
   My close attention drew;
O'er two, the tall grass, bending, sighed,
   But one seemed fresh and new.

As lingering there, I mused awhile
   On death's long, dreamless sleep;
And opening life's deceitful smile,
   A mourner came to weep.

Her form was bowed, but not with years,
　　Her words were faint and few,
And on those little graves, her tears
　　Distilled like evening dew.


A prattling boy, some four years old,
　　Her trembling hand embraced,
And from my heart, the tale he told
　　Will never be effaced.


"Mamma, now you must love me more,
　　For little sister's dead.
And t' other sister died before,
　　And brother, too, you said.


"Mamma, what made sweet sister die?
　　She loved me when we played;
You told me if I would not cry,
　　You'd show me where she's laid."


"'Tis here, my child, that sister lies,
　　Deep buried in the ground,
No light comes to her little eyes,
　　And she can hear no sound."


"Mamma, why can't we take her up,
　　And put her in my bed?
I'll feed her from my little cup,
　　And then she won't be dead.

" For sister 'll be afraid to lie
　In this dark grave to-night,
And she 'll be very cold, and cry
　Because there is no light."

" No, sister is not cold, my child,
　For God, who saw her die,
As he looked down from heaven, and smiled,
　Recalled her to the sky ;

" And then, her spirit quickly fled
　To God, by whom 't was given ;
Her body, in the ground is dead,
　But sister lives in heaven."

" Mamma, won't she be hungry there,
　And want some bread to eat ?
And who will give her clothes to wear,
　And keep them clean and neat ?

" Papa must go and carry some,
　I 'll send her all I 've got ;
And he must bring sweet sister home,
　Mamma, now must he not ? "

" No, my dear child, that cannot be,
　But if you 're good and true,
You 'll one day go to her, but she
　Can never come to you.

" ' Let little children come to me,'
　Once our good Saviour said,
And in his arms she 'll always be,
　And God will give her bread."

## THE FAMILY.

THE family is like a book:
　　The children are the leaves,
The parents are the covers,
　　That protective beauty give.

At first, the pages of the book
　　Are blank, and purely fair,
But time soon writeth memories,
　　And painteth pictures there.

Love, is the little golden clasp,
　　That bindeth up the trust,
Oh, break it not, lest all the leaves
　　Should scatter and be lost.

CARY.

## THE STORY OF THE LITTLE RID HIN.

THERE was, onc't upon a time,
　　A little shmall rid hin,
Off in the good ould counthry,
　　Where yees ha' niver bin.

Nice and quiet, shure she was,
　　An' niver did any harram;
She lived alane all by herself,
　　An' worked upon her farram.

There lived, out o'er the hill,
  In a great din o' rocks,
A crafty, shly, an' wicked
  Ould felly iv a fox.

This rashkill iv a fox,
  He tuk it in his head,
He 'd have the little shmall rid hin,
  So, whin he wint to bed,

He laid awake, an' thaught,
  What a foine thing 't wad be
To fetch her home, an' bile her up,
  For his ould marm an' he.

An' so he thaught, an' thaught,
  Until he grew so thin,
That there was nothing lift of him,
  But jist his bones and shkin.

But the shmall rid hin was wise,
  She always locked her door,
An' in her pocket pit the key,
  To keep the fox out, shure.

But at last, there came a schame
  Intil his wicked head,
An' so he tuk a great big bag,
  An' to his mither said,—

"Now have the pot all bilin'
  Agin the time I come;
We 'll ate the shmall rid hin to-night,
  For shure I 'll bring her home."

An' so away he wint,
  Wid the bag upon his back,
An' up the hill, an' through the woods,
  Saftly he made his thrack.

An' thin he came alang,
  Crapin' as shtill 's a mouse,
To where the little shmall rid hin
  Lived in her shnug ould house.

An' out she comes hersel'
  Jist as he got in sight,
To pick up shticks to make her fire;
  "Aha!" says fox, "all right.

" Begorra, now, I 'll have yees
  Widout much throuble more;"
An' in he shlips quite unbeknownst,
  An' hides be'ind the door.

An' thin, a minute afther,
  In comes the shmall rid hin,
An' shuts the door, an' locks it too,
  An' thinks, "I 'm safely in."

An' thin she tarns around,
  An' looks be'ind the door;
There shtands the fox, wid his big tail
  Shpread out upon the floor.

Dear me! she was so shcared
  Wid such a wondrous sight,
She dropped her apron full of shticks,
  An' flew up in a fright,

An' lighted on the bame,
    Across on top the room;
"Aha!" says she, "ye don't have me,
    Ye may as well go home."

"Aha!" says fox, "we'll see,
    I'll fetch yees down from that;"
So out he marched upon the floor,
    Right under where she sat.

And thin he whirreld around,
    An' round, an' round, an' round,
Fashter, an' fashter, an' fashter,
    Afther his tail on the ground.

Until the shmall rid hin,
    She got so dizzy shure,
Wid looking at the fox's tail,
    She jist dropped on the floor.

An' fox, he whipped her up,
    An' pit her in his bag,
An' off he shtarted all alane,
    Him an' his little dag.

All day he thracked the woods,
    Up-hill an' down again;
An' wid him smotherin' in the bag,
    The little shmall rid hin.

Sorra a know she knowed,
    Awhere she was that day;
Says she, "I'm biled an' ate up, shure,
    An' what'll be to pay?"

Thin she betho't hersel,
     An' tuk her shissors out,
An' shnipped a big hole in the bag,
     So she could look about.

An' 'fore ould fox could think,
     She lept right out — she did,
An' thin picked up a great big shtone,
     And popped it in instid.

An' then she rins off home,
     Her outside door she locks;
Thinks she, "You see you don't have me,
     You crafty, shly ould fox."

An' fox, he tugged away
     Wid the great, big, hivy shtone,
Thimpin' his shoulders very bad,
     As he wint on alone.

An' whin he came in sight,
     O' his great din o' rocks,
Jist watchin' for him at the door,
     He shpied ould mither fox.

"Have ye the pot a bilin'?"
     Says he to ould fox thin;
"Shure an' it is, me child," says she;
     "Have ye the shmall rid hin?"

"Yes, just here in my bag,
     As shure as I shtand here;
Open the lid till I pit her in;
     Open it — niver fear."

So the rashkill cut the sthring,
 An' hild the big bag over;
"Now when I shake her in," says he,
 "Do ye pit on the cover."

"Yis, that I will;" an' thin
 The shtone wint in wid a dash,
An' the pot o' bilin' water
 Came over thim — ker-splash,

An' shcalted them both to death,
 So they could n't breathe no more;
An' the little shmall rid hin lived safe
 Jist where she lived before.

    Versified by F. W. SWEETSER, *Riverside Magazine.*

————◆————

## THE FAMOUS BATTLE OF BUMBLE–BUG AND BUMBLE-BEE.

BUMBLE–BUG and Bumble-Bee
 Agreed to fight a battle;
For Bumble-Bug said Bumble-Bee
 Had lighted on his apple.
So Bumble-Bug to Bumble-Bee
 Cried out, "Come, sir, right down,
Or I will take you on my horns,
 And toss you out of town."

But Bumble-Bee told Bumble-Bug
 Apples were his to eat;
And bade the Buggy get away
 With all his little feet.

Then Bumble-Bug began to swell,
  And Bumble-Bee to buzz,
And soon they had their little heads
  All in a little fuzz.


And Bumble-Bug began to climb
  The apple round and red,
And as he went a-bugging up
  To Bumble-Bee he said:
"I'll show you, sir, old Bumble-Bee,
  Whose apple you are eating;
I'll push you off upon the ground,
  And give you, sir, a beating."


Then Bumble-Bee and Bumble-Bug
  Begin their famous battle,
And soon both tumble headlong down,
  From off the big, round apple.
But Bumble-Bug soon scrabbles up
  And opens wide his eyes;
And Bumble-Bee shakes out his wings
  And at Sir Buggy flies.


The Bumble-Bug tried hard to scratch,
  The Bumble-Bee to sting;
The Bee put out the Buggy's eye,
  The Bug tore off Bee's wing.
Then Bumble-Bug and Bumble-Bee
  Each took a little rest;
Sir Bug laid down upon his back,
  Sir Bee upon his breast.

"Come, Bumble-Bug," said Bumble-Bee,
  "Let's talk this matter over,
As we are resting here a bit,
  Under this shady clover."
"'T was all your fault!" said Bumble-Bug;
  "'T was yours!" buzzed Bumble-Bee;
"I found the apple first," said Bug,
  "Under the apple-tree."

"Ah, ha! ah, ha!" cried Bumble-Bee,
  "Just like a great black bug!
I'll warrant, you from out the ground
  Your dinners oft have dug;
But I — I found the apple
  Up in the apple-tree;
I get my dinners clean and sweet, —
  I am a Bumble-Bee."

Then Bumble-Bug said he 'd get up
  And kill the Bee outright;
And Bumble-Bee began to buzz,
  All ready for the fight.
Oh, 't was a fearful sight to see,
  As Bug, with lifted horns,
Went dash with all his might at Bee,
  With great, black, shining horns!

Just then a tiny Ant spoke out
  From off her little hill,
And said: "Alas! most noble sirs,
  My heart with grief you fill,

To see a Bumble-Bee and Bug,
  As like as any brothers,
Go scratch and sting, at eye and wing,
  Till each has spoiled the other's!

"The apple, big, and round, and red,
  Is, sure, enough for all;
'T would last a little Ant like me
  The summer and the fall.
There Bumble-Bee could sip the juice,
  While Buggy nibbed the skin,
And I, with hundred other Ants,
  Could tid-bit out and in.

"'T is yours, 't is mine; behold how fair,
  With wealth for each untold, —
This rounded sphere of juicy pulp,
  This rind of red and gold!
How pleasant, too, as we have read,
  How good a thing 't would be,
Together as a family
  To dwell in unity."

Then Bumble-Bug and Bumble-Bee
  Were very much ashamed,
While thus the quiet little Ant
  Their wicked conduct blamed;
And tears stood in that flashing eye,
  Down drooped that vaunting wing,
As each pledged never more
  Do such a naughty thing.

But not the tear in Buggy's eye,
　　Nor Bumble's drooping wing,
Can take from out their little hearts,
　　Remembered scratch and sting.
And ever, when they meet again
　　On pretty fruit or flower,
They think, with still repentant hearts
　　Upon that battle hour.

　　　　　　Mrs. J. W. Hoyt, in *Riverside Magazine.*

———◆———

## THE WONDERFUL SACK.

THE apple-boughs half hid the house
　　Where lived the lonely widow;
Behind it stood the chestnut wood,
　　Before it spread the meadow.

She had no money in her till,
　　She was too poor to borrow;
With her lame leg she could not beg;
　　And no one cheered her sorrow.

She had no wood to cook her food,
　　And but one chair to sit in;
Last spring she lost a cow, that cost
　　A whole year's steady knitting.

She had worn her fingers to the bone,
　　Her back was growing double;
One day the pig tore up her wig, —
　　But that's not half her trouble.

Her best black gown was faded brown,
  Her shoes were all in tatters,
With not a pair for Sunday wear:
  Said she, "It little matters!

"Nobody asks me now to ride,
  My garments are not fitting;
And with my crutch I care not much
  To hobble off to meeting.

"I still preserve my Testament;
  And though the *Acts* are missing,
And *Luke* is torn, and *Hebrews* worn,
  On Sunday 't is a blessing.

"And other days I open it
  Before me on the table,
And there I sit, and read, and knit,
  As long as I am able."

One evening she had closed the book,
  But still she sat there knitting;
"Meow-meow!" complained the old black cat;
  "Mew-mew!" the spotted kitten.

And on the hearth, with sober mirth,
  "Chirp, chirp!" replied the cricket.
'Twas dark,—but hark! "Bow-ow!" the bark
  Of Ranger at the wicket!

"Is Ranger barking at the moon?
  Or what can be the matter?
What trouble now?"  "Bow-ow! bow-ow!"—
  She hears the old gate clatter.

"It is the wind that bangs the gate,
  And I must knit my stocking!"
But hush! — what's that? Rat-tat, rat-tat!
  Alas! there's some one knocking!

"Dear me! dear me! who can it be?
  Where, where is my crutch-handle?"
She rubs a match with hasty scratch, —
  She cannot light the candle!

Rat-tat! scratch, scratch! the worthless match!
  The cat growls in the corner,
Rat-tat! scratch, scratch! up flies the latch, —
  "Good-evening, Mrs. Warner!"

The kitten spits and lifts her back,
  Her eyes glare on the stranger;
The old cat's tail ruffs big and black,
  Loud barks the old dog Ranger!

Blue burns at last the tardy match,
  And dim the candle glimmers;
Along the floor, beside the door,
  The cold white moonlight glimmers.

"Sit down!" The widow gives her chair,
  "Get out!" she says to Ranger;
"Alas! I do not know your name."
  "No matter!" quoth the stranger.

His limbs are strong, his beard is long,
  His hair is dark and wavy;
Upon his back he bears a sack, —
  His staff is stout and heavy.

"My way is lost, and with the frost
    I feel my fingers tingle."
Then from his back he slips the sack,
    Ho! did you hear it jingle?

"Nay, keep your chair; while you sit there,
    I'll take the other corner."
"I'm sorry, sir, I have no fire!"
    "No matter, Mrs. Warner!"

He shakes the sack,—the magic sack!
    Amazed the widow gazes!
Ho, ho! the chimney's full of wood!
    Ha, ha! the wood it blazes!

Ho, ho! ha, ha! the merry fire!
    It sputters and it crackles!
Snap, snap! flash, flash! old oak and ash
    Send out a million sparkles.

The stranger sits upon his sack
    . Beside the chimney-corner,
And rubs his hands before the brands,
    And smiles on Mrs. Warner.

She feels her heart beat fast with fear,
    But what can be the danger?
"Can I do aught for you, kind sir?"
    "I'm hungry!" quoth the stranger.

"Alas!" she said, "I have no food
    For boiling, or for baking!"
"I've food," quoth he, "for you and me!"
    And gave his sack a shaking.

Out rattled knives, and forks, and spoons!
  Twelve eggs, potatoes plenty!
One large soup-dish, two plates of fish,
  And bread enough for twenty!

And Rachel, calming her surprise,
  As well as she was able,
Saw, following these, two roasted geese,
  A tea-urn, and a table!

Strange, was it not? each dish was hot!
  Not even a plate was broken;
The cloth was laid, and all arrayed,
  Before a word was spoken!

"Sit up! sit up! and we will sup,
  Dear Madam, while we're able!"
Said she, "The room is poor and small
  For such a famous table!"

Again the stranger shakes the sack,
  The walls begin to rumble!
Another shake! the rafters quake!
  You'd think the roof would tumble!

Shake, shake! The room grows high and large,
  The walls are painted over!
Shake, shake! Out fall four chairs in all,
  A bureau, and a sofa!

The stranger stops to wipe the sweat
  That down his face is streaming;
"Sit up, sit up! and we will sup,"
  Quoth he, "while all is steaming!"

The widow hobbled on her crutch,
  He kindly sprang to aid her;
"All this," said she, "is too much for me!"
  Quoth he, "We'll have a waiter!"

Shake, shake, once more! and from the sack,
  Out popped a little fellow,
With elbows bare, bright eyes, sleek hair,
  And trousers striped with yellow.

His legs were short, his body plump,
  His cheek was like a cherry;
He turned three times; he gave a jump;
  His laugh rang loud and merry!

He placed his hand upon his heart,
  And scraped and bowed so handy!
"Your humble servant, sir," he said,
  Like any little dandy.

The widow laughed, a long, loud laugh,
  And up she started, screaming;
When ho! and lo! the room was dark!
  She'd been asleep and dreaming!

The stranger and his magic sack,
  The dishes, and the fishes,
The geese and things, had taken wings,
  Like riches, or like witches!

All, all was gone! she sat alone;
  Her hands had dropped their knitting;
"Meow, meow!" the cat upon the mat;
  "Mew-mew! mew-mew!" the kitten.

The hearth is bleak, — and hark! the creak! —
  "Chirp, chirp!" the lonesome cricket;
" Bow-ow!" says Ranger to the moon;
  The wind is at the wicket.

And still she sits, and as she knits,
  She ponders o'er the vision;
"I saw it written on the sack, —
  'A CHEERFUL DISPOSITION.'

" I know God sent the dream, and meant
  To teach this useful lesson,
That out of peace, and pure content
  Springs every earthly blessing!"

Said she, "I 'll make the sack my own!
  I 'll shake away all sorrow!"
She shook the sack for me to-day;
  She 'll shake for you to-morrow.

She shakes out hope, and joy, and peace,
  And happiness comes after;
She shakes out smiles for all the world;
  She shakes out love and laughter.

For poor and rich, — no matter which, —
  For young folks, or for old folks;
For strong and weak, for proud and meek,
  For warm folks, and for cold folks;

For children coming home from school,
  And sometimes for the teacher;
For white and black, she shakes the sack, —
  In short, for every creature.

And everybody who has grief,
  The sufferer and the mourner,
From far and near, come now to hear
  Kind words from Mrs. Warner.

They go to her with heavy hearts,
  They come away with light ones;
They go to her with cloudy brows,
  They come away with bright ones.

All love her well, and I could tell
  Of many a cheering present
Of fruits and things, their friendship brings,
  To make her fireside pleasant.

She always keeps a cheery fire;
  Her house is painted over;
She has food in store, and chairs for four,
  A bureau, and a sofa.

She says these seem just like her dream,
  And tells again the vision:
"I saw it written on the sack, —
  'A Cheerful Disposition.'"

J. T. TROWBRIDGE, in *The Vagabonds and Other Poems.*

## THE FACTOR.

[A quaint ditty of ye olden time, as repeated by Mrs. OLIVE WHITNEY in 1840.]

BEHOLD here a ditty, the truth is no jest,
Concerning a gentleman who lived in the east,
Who by his great gaming came to poverty,
And after that, went many voyages to sea.

He was well instructed; a man of great wit;
Three merchants in London all thinking it fit,
They made him their captain, and factor also,
And he with them a voyage to Turkey did go.

As he walked the streets in Turkey, he found
A poor man's dead body, that lay on the ground;
He asked the reason that made it there lie,
And one of the natives made to him this reply:

"This man was a Christian, sir, while he drew breath;
His debts being unpaid, he lies here above earth."
"Oh, what was the debt?" the factor he cried!
"Fifty pounds, sir, it was," the native replied.

"That is a large sum," said the factor, "indeed,
But to see him lie here makes my heart for to bleed;"
So then by the factor the money was paid,
And into a grave the dead body was laid.

And as he walked farther, by chance he did spy
A beautiful damsel just going for to die,
A young waiting-maiden, who hanged must be,
For naught but offending a Turkish ladie.

He heard what the crime was; it filled him with strife,
Saying, "What shall I give for this young creature's life?"
The answer returned him was, "A hundred pound,"
Which he for her pardon did freely lay down.

He said, "Come, fair creature your weeping refrain,
And be of good comfort, you shall not be slain:
I've purchased your pardon, and therefore wilt thee
Be willing to go to England with me?"

She said, "Yes, sir, I thank you, you've freed me from death;
I'm bound for to love you as long as I've breath,
And with you to England I'm willing to go,
And due respect to you till death I will show."

He brought her to England, and, as it is said,
He set up housekeeping, and made her his maid;
In everything finding her faithful and just,
With the keys of his riches he did her entrust.

At length this young factor was hired once more,
To cross the great waves where the billows did roar,
And into that country his course was to steer,
Of which his maid's father was governor, we hear.

It being a hot country, then he did prepare
Some thinly clothing for that country wear;
He bought a silk waistcoat; and, as it is told,
His housekeeper wrought it with silver and gold.

She said to him, "Sir, I now understand
You are going, factor, into such a land;
And if you to that prince's court enter in,
I pray you let this flowered garment be seen."

He said, "To that prince's court now I must go ;
The meaning of your words I'd be glad for to know."
"I'd rather not tell you ; some reason you'll find."
"With that, ma'am," said he, "I'll fulfill your mind."

He sailed away, and he came to that port,
And straightway he went to the emperor's court ;
And it was the custom sometimes in that place·
For to present some noble gifts to his grace.

His gift was accepted, and as he stood by,
On that flowered garment the prince cast his eye,
Which caused him to wonder, and thus he did say,
"Who wrought you this garment ?  Oh, tell me, I pray !"

He said, "The last time I was in Turkey
I saw a young lady who hanged must be,
And to save her life gave a hundred pound,
And brought her with me to fair London  town.

"She is my housekeeper while I'm in this land,
And, when at my coming she did understand,
She wrought this garment and gave charge to me,
To let it be seen by your great majesty."

The prince he replied, "This robe that I wear
Is of the same color and spot, I declare ;
Your maid wrought them both, and she's my daughter dear ;
I have not heard from her this many a year.

"For to pay a visit to a neighboring prince
We sent her in a ship, and hain't heard from her since ;
We feared the ocean had proved her grave,
But it seems that in Turkey she was taken a slave.

"Many a tear in my court has been shed
For the loss of my child, whom we thought had been dead.
The princess, her mother, for her could not rest,
And tears drew many a sigh from her breast.

"Your ship shall be richly loaded with speed,
And I will send for her a convoy indeed;
Because out of pity you saved my child's life,
Bring her alive to me and she may be your wife.

"But if you don't live to bring her to me,
The man who brings her to me his wife she shall be;
And twenty-five hundred a year you shall have
For being so kind as my child's life to save."

The wind being fair, he sailed away
In the same ship her father sent for her convey;
And home to the city of London did go,
And gave this young lady these tidings to know.

He said, "Noble lady, I've good news to tell—
The princes, your father and mother, are well;
And your noble parents this thing designed,
In the bands of wedlock we two shall be jined.

"But perhaps, noble lady, you will not agree
To marry a poor man, especially me."
She said, "Were you a beggar I would be your wife,
Because when just dying you saved my life.

"I ne'er shall forget that great token of love,
And of all men breathing I prize you above;
And since it's so ordered, I'm well pleased now,
And am glad that my parents will this thing allow.

"Come, sell off the goods that we have now in store,
And give all the money to those that are poor;
And let us be journeying over the main,
I long for to see my dear parents again."

This thing was soon done, and they sailed away,
In the same ship her father sent for her convey;
But mark what was done on the ocean wide,
To deprive this young factor of his noble bride.

The factor, one night, as he lay asleep,
The captain, who conveyed them over the deep,
The ship being under sail, overboard did him throw,
Saying, "Now I shall have this young lady, I know."

There happened to be a small island at hand
To which he did swim to, as we understand,
And there we will leave him for awhile to mourn,
And unto the captain and ship we'll return.

And then, the next morning, when daylight did peep,
He waked this young lady from out of her sleep;
He said, "Noble lady, the factor's not here,
He's fell overboard and is drowned, we fear."

To hear this sad news, the tears they did flow;
He said, "Noble lady, now since it is so,
There's none here can help it, so don't troubled be;
In two or three days, and your parents you'll see."

Soon they arrived at the destined port;
This lady went weeping to her father's court,
Where she was received with joy and great mirth,
Saying, "Where is the man who has freed you from death?"

The captain replied, "As he lay asleep,
He fell overboard, and was drowned in the deep;
Your grace said the man whom your daughter would bring
Should have her, and I hope you'll perform this thing."

"Yes, that was my promise," the prince he replied;
"What sayest thou, daughter; wilt thou be his bride?"
She said, "Yes, my dear father; but yet, if you please,
For the man who saved my life let me mourn forty days."

So into close mourning this lady she went,
For the loss of her best friend in tears to lament;
And there we will leave her to mourn for awhile,
And return to the factor, who was left on the isle.

On that desert island the factor he lay
In floods of tears weeping, two nights and a day;
And then, the next thing that appeared to his view,
Was a little old man paddling in a canoe.

The factor called to him, which caused him to stay,
And, when coming near him, the old man did say,
"Friend, how came you here?" the tears they did flow,
He told him the secret, and where he would go.

He said, "If you'll promise, and be true to me,
And give me the first child born unto thee,
When it's twenty months old, to that port I'll you bring;
I will not release you without that very thing."

The factor considered the thing would cause grief;
But since, as without it, there was no relief,
He said, "Life it is sweet, and my life for to save,
Carry me to that port, and your will you shall have."

Soon they arrived at that port, and when
Coming near to the gate, he saw his lady then
Looking out at the window, and seeing him there,
From sorrow to great joy transported they were.

Then into the court with joy he was received,
His lady soon met him who for him had so grieved;
She said, "My jewel, my joy, my dear,
Why you 've so long tarried, oh, pray let me hear."

Why he 'd so long tarried, then he did relate,
And by what means he came to her father's gate;
He said, "I was thrown overboard in my sleep,
And it was the captain who threw me in the deep."

The captain was sent for, who came with all speed,
But seeing the factor, who was there indeed,
He showed himself guilty, and, like a great knave
Leaped into the ocean, which proved his grave.

And then, the next day, in triumph, we find,
The factor and lady in wedlock are jined;
And then in the compass and space of three years,
They have a fine son and a daughter, we hears.

The son was the first born, a perfect beautie,
He was well beloved by the whole familie;
When 't was twenty months old came the man for the child
Who delivered the factor from that desert isle.

The factor he saw him, the tears they did flow,
He gave this young lady and her parents to know
He was forced to make that promise, or lie
On that desert isle till with hunger to die.

Then this grim ghost he soon did appear,
Which made the court tremble, and filled them with fear;
They said one to another, "Sure, this is no man,
For to save our darling, let's do what we can."

The grim ghost replied, "I must have my due,
There's one babe for me, and another for you;
I must have the first-born, so give it to me;"
With that the whole family wept bitterlie.

The babe's mother took it, and many tears fell,
And, when she had kissed it, she bid it farewell,
Saying, "'T is all for the sake of my husband, that I
Do part with my first-born, though for it I die."

The grim ghost did turn to the factor and say,
"Sir, don't you remember, in Turkey, one day
You saw a dead body that lay on the ground,
And to have it buried you gave fifty pound?

"Sir, I am the spirit of that dead bodie,
I saved your life for your love shown to me;
Now you may keep your babes, and the Lord bless you
                all;"
And straightway he vanished out of the hall.

And there we will leave them in joy and in mirth,
To love one another while God gives them breath;
And thus by the factor and lady, you see
There's none can prevent what God doth decree.

# THE CHAMPION JUMPER.

THERE was a man in Hoppertown
   Who used to jump so high.
He kept a cushion on his head
   Lest he should hit the sky.

But still on jumping he was bent.
   And one day jumped so far
He missed the path to Mother Earth.
   And landed on a star.

Then. after resting him a bit.
   He said. " 'T is very plain.
The more I jump. the more I may.
   So I will try again."

He spied the " Goat." and with a bound
   He lighted on his back;
Harnessed the " Dragon " to the " Plough."
   Pursued the " Lion's " track.

On " Pegasus " he swiftly rode:
   On " Aquilla " he flew:
The " Ram " he captured by the horns:
   Bestrode old " Taurus " too.

Like grasshoppers, his legs became :
   His strength no limit knew:
I think each star he 'll visit yet.
   That shines in upper blue.

And now, dear little girls and boys,
    If you will use your eyes,
And do not go to bed too soon,
    You 'll see him in the skies.


For, on these pleasant autumn nights,
    What we call shooting-stars,
Are but the leaps this man doth make,
    Who jumped from Earth to Mars.

JENNY WALLIS in *Harper's Young People.*


——•——


## THE CHAMPION JUMPER AS A TEACHER.

A DARING rider once bestrode
    Each fiery constellation ;
And, since that day, his fearless deeds
    Fill us with admiration.


This man, who used his nimble legs
    In leaping through the skies,
Returned, one day, to Hoppertown,
    The wisest of the wise.


Through all the nations of the earth
    His fame spread far and wide :
In Europe, Asia, Africa,
    And in the isles beside.

Astronomers from distant lands
  Came flocking to his door:
And kings forsook their thrones to see
  A man who thus could soar.

The sparkling gems from other worlds
  The kings beheld with awe :
Such jewels ne'er were found on earth,
  And mortals never saw.

They poured their treasures at his feet,
  Begging that he would spare
A few of all these precious stones
  Upon their crowns to wear.

" In vain," he cried. " you offer gold,
  I 've more than all you own ;
These priceless gems I would not sell
  To sit upon a throne."

Then all th' astronomers and kings
  Turned gray with wild despair :
The youngest head among them all
  Was crowned with silvered hair.

But, while they sat with gloom oppressed,
  He bent his head in thought :
Then raised it with a beaming smile,
  A smile with meaning fraught.

" 'T is true," he said, " I cannot sell
  These treasures from the skies ;
But for your *love* I 'll teach you how
  Yourselves to win the prize."

" Then here 's my hand—your faithful friend,"
  Each king of earth replied;
" And we are yours for earth or sky,"
  Each learned savant cried.

His pupils then they all became,
  And—as their courage grew—
He led the way—they followed fast;
  He kept his promise true.

At first across a river wide,
  And then across an ocean,
They leaped, as he the secret taught,
  Raising a great commotion.

Each day they gathered up their robes
  And leaped a trifle higher;
—A trifle was a million rods;
  A trillion would be nigher.—

Within a week they gained the moon
  And wandered o'er its mountains;
And chatted with the old man there,
  While sitting by its fountains.

Within a month their teacher said:
  " Your legs have grown so supple,
I think a longer trip we 'll take
  In one week or a couple."

At length the wished-for day arrived
  When they should scale the skies,
And for themselves should visit worlds
  No eye on earth descries.

Their careful training now they proved,
　And well the strain they bore ;
Yet their good teacher, strong and brave,
　Arrived an hour before.

" Well done ! " he cried, " pray heed it not
　That I should prove the winner ;
Compose yourselves and rest awhile,
　You 'll be my guests for dinner."

Then, seating all his loyal friends
　On Saturn's glowing ring,
He bade them listen to the notes
　The gladsome planets sing.

A mammoth ox, well filled with spice,
　Was browning while they rested ;
The welcome odor it gave forth
　A toothsome meal suggested.

From milky way the comets brought
　All the rich drink they wanted ;
And brilliant meteors danced around,
　Like valets all undaunted.

The ring was wide whereon they sat,
　While, resting firm on Saturn,
A smaller ring their table served,
　Of most convenient pattern.

A jollier circle ne'er was found
　Than feasted at that table ;
And each the merriest stories told
　Of which such men are able.

Refreshed in mind and body too
    They viewed the heavens over,
Grasping with fondest love his hand
    Whose skill made each a rover.

These famous men are still abroad ;
    The kings each chose a star,
And quite content a world to rule,
    Wish not their thrones afar.

Th' astronomers are happier still ;
    No longer through a glass
They scrutinize the distant worlds,—
    Their dreams have come to pass.

We may not live to see the day,
    But I am sure these sages
A wondrous book will one day write ;
    May I but turn its pages!

In Hoppertown the tale I tell
    Is whispered still at eve ;
To some it seems an idle dream,—
    Others its truth believe.

                JENNY WALLIS.

# THE BLACKBERRY GIRL.

" WHY, Phebe, have you come so soon ?
  Where are your berries, child ?
You cannot, sure, have sold them all ;
  You had a basket piled."

" No, mother; as I climbed a fence,
  The nearest way to town,
My apron caught upon a stake,
  And so I tumbled down.

" I scratched my arm and tore my hair,
  But still did not complain ;
And, had my blackberries been safe,
  Should not have cared a grain.

" But when I saw them on the ground,
  All scattered by my side,
I picked my empty basket up,
  And down I sat, and cried.

" Just then a pretty little miss
  Chanced to be walking by :
She stopped, and, looking pitiful,
  She begged me not to cry.

"' Poor little girl, you fell,' said she,
  ' And must be sadly hurt.'
' Oh, no,' I cried ; ' but see my fruit —
  All mixed with sand and dirt.'

"' Well, do not grieve for that,' she said ;
  ' Go home and get some more.'
' Ah, no ; for I have stripped the vines ;
  These were the last they bore. `

"' My father, miss, is very poor,
  And works in yonder stall ;
He has so many little ones,
  He cannot clothe us all.

"' I always longed to go to church,
  But never could I go ;
For, when I asked him for a gown,
  He always answered, " No.

"' " There 's not a father in the world
  That loves his children more ;
I 'd get you one, with all my heart,
  But, Phebe, I am poor."

"' But when the blackberries were ripe,
  He said to me, one day,
" Phebe, if you will take the time
  That 's given you for play,

"' " And gather blackberries enough,
  And carry them to town,
To buy your bonnet and your shoes,
  *I 'll* try to get a gown."

" ' O, miss, I fairly jumped for joy,
    My spirits were so light;
And so, when I had leave to play,
    I picked with all my might.

" ' I sold enough to get my shoes,
    About a week ago;
And these, if they had not been spilt,
    Would buy a bonnet, too.

" ' But now they're gone, they all are gone,
    And I can get no more;
And Sundays I must stay at home,
    Just as I did before.'

" And, mother, then I cried again,
    As hard as I could cry;
And, looking up, I saw a tear
    Was standing in her eye.

" She took her bonnet from her head, —
    ' Here, here!' she cried, ' take this!'
' Oh, no, indeed; I fear your ma
    Would be offended, miss.'

" ' My ma! no, never! she delights
    All sorrow to beguile;
And 't is the sweetest joy she feels,
    To make the wretched smile.

" ' She taught me, when I had enough,
    To share it with the poor,
And never let a needy child
    Go empty from the door.

"' So, take it; for you need not fear
  Offending her, you see;
I have another, too, at home;
  And one 's enough for me.'

"So then I took it; here it is;
  For, pray, what could I do?
And, mother, I shall love that miss
  As long as I love you."

# INDEX TO TITLES.

# INDEX TO FIRST LINES.